BITOPIA

ARI MAGNUSSON

OLIVANDER PRESS
BOSTON

For my brilliant, shining suns, Oliver and Anders,
and my perpetually bright blue sky, Royce

CHAPTER 1

Stewart ran through the neighborhood, clutching his backpack to his chest. He cut across the lawns of houses, pumping his legs furiously, using the bushes and trees dotting the yards for cover. They were somewhere behind him, and they were coming. For him.

The old trees lining the streets, with their gnarled trunks and creaking canopies of spindly, twisting branches, towered over him as he sped past. Adults weren't home from work yet, and Stewart had raced out of his sixth-grade classroom and through the doors of the Oak Hill School the moment the bell had rung, so he was well ahead of the other students. The neighborhood was deserted.

As he ran, Stewart tried his best to ignore the darkened windows of the empty houses. He had dreams where he was running through the neighborhood, and the faces of his pursuers would appear like ghostly apparitions behind the glass, their mouths twisted in evil sneers, letting him know that his attempts to escape were futile. Stewart squeezed his backpack tighter as he ran. No matter what happened, he couldn't let them catch him. If they did, they would certainly find what he was carrying in his pack. And if *that* happened...

Stewart forced the thought from his head and pushed on. At the corner of Maple Street and Birch Street, he slid under a big green hemlock bush, disappearing completely beneath the bottom branches.

He lay panting on the dirt, listening. At first he could only hear the pounding of his heart and his own gasping, but as his breathing slowed, the sounds of the neighborhood became audible. A faint breeze whispered through the trees, rustling leaves and swaying small branches. From a few blocks away, the sound of a passing car emerged from the stillness, then faded back to silence. Far away, he heard the rumble and rattle of a construction site.

Stewart closed his eyes, trying to shut down all senses except for his hearing. He took in every vibration, every whisper of noise, sorting through them, trying to discern the telltale sound of his pursuers. And then he heard it. Almost as quiet as the flapping of a butterfly's wings, he detected the sound he dreaded most: the faint hum of knobby tires on pavement. It was barely perceptible, but over the months since he started at his new school, his ears had become attuned to the noise.

As he listened, he heard a *zip-zop, zip-zop, zip-zop*, the sound of the hum stopping and then starting again. They were jumping the curbs at the driveways. But more importantly, what the sound told him was that Dirk, Frankie, and Judd, the bullies of the Oak Hill School who called themselves "the Rage"—a dumb name to be sure, but not something that Stewart or anyone else for that matter would dare tell them—were all riding together. And as long as they were all behind him, his way forward would be clear.

He scrambled out from under the hemlock and sprinted toward Ricrac Road, a busy thoroughfare lined with shops that curved around the base of a hill. Just one block down Ricrac was Elm Street, where Stewart lived. Ricrac was usually the safest way home, thanks to the occasional adult walking past on the sidewalk, which was enough to keep the Rage at bay. All he would have to do is make it down the block and up the hill to his house, and he and his backpack would be safe.

As Stewart approached the corner of Maple and Ricrac, the sounds of the construction site that he had heard from under the hemlock grew louder. When he reached the corner, he skidded to a stop behind a large maple tree and stared. Trucks, backhoes, and men wearing orange vests and hardhats were crawling across the entire width of the road. Every few moments, the rapid thumping of a jackhammer would fill the air, masking all sounds except for the clomping of rocks and pieces of asphalt dropped by a backhoe digger into a dump truck. The blacktop was pockmarked with holes and trenches. The grate of a storm drain had been pulled off and was lying next to the curb. The whole area had been cordoned off with a long yellow caution tape strung between white plastic sawhorses.

Stewart's heart leapt with relief. With all the construction workers around, the Rage would leave him alone. He could stroll down the sidewalk as carefree as the mayor. But then the backhoe engine shut off and the jackhammer went quiet. Stewart realized that the workers moving about were actually putting away shovels and tools. One by one they climbed into cars and trucks parked at the edge of the site and drove off. Before long, the place was deserted.

Stewart's hopes sank almost as fast as his fears rose. He was once again alone. No one was there to drive the bullies away.

Knowing that the Rage was getting closer with each passing second, he gritted his teeth and dashed out into the open street to cross. He braced himself for the inevitable whoops and howls that the Rage would make when they saw him. But the shouts didn't come.

Stewart leapt to the far curb, took cover behind an old oak tree, and slowly peered around the gnarled trunk. The bullies were nowhere in sight. He listened, but couldn't hear the sound of the tires. Where had they gone? He sank back against the trunk, fighting a feeling of panic. Not knowing where they were meant that he was vulnerable. For all he knew, they were circling the block, heading up the hill and coming down the other side, which would cut him off.

Stewart checked the zippers of his backpack to make sure the cargo was safe. Tucked deep inside were five old coins: two silver quarters, a silver dime, a Buffalo nickel, and an Indian Head penny from the 1800s. They had been his grandfather's, and together they were worth over one hundred dollars. If the Rage found them, they were as good as gone.

Stewart peered around the oak tree again. He thought about backtracking, circling around behind the Rage and going up the hill to Elm; however, that route was much longer and there was no chance of an adult being around to help him. At least Ricrac offered the chance of a grown-up out shopping. He would take his chances on Ricrac.

Like a prowling cat, Stewart crept slowly along the sidewalk, keeping as close as he could to the storefronts, studying the way forward and looking back over his shoulder in case the Rage appeared. He passed the card shop, the flower shop, the drug store, the post office. He was halfway there. Dress shop, coffee shop, Italian deli. The sign for Elm Street was almost in view.

Finally he saw the corner bookstore and Elm Street. He was about to charge forward when he heard the dreaded hum. It quickly grew louder and was much higher in pitch, meaning the bullies were speeding down the Elm Street hill. In only a few seconds, they would round the corner onto Ricrac. Stewart turned to flee back to Maple Street but stopped cold. Sitting nonchalantly on his bike at the end of the block was Frankie. Behind him, Stewart heard two bikes skid to a stop.

CHAPTER 2

"Well, look who it is," Frankie said, his voice menacing.

"Hello, pipsqueak," Stewart heard Judd say behind him.

Stewart's knees started to shake. The bullies, who were in the eighth grade, were tall and muscular, with broad chests and sinewy arms. Judd, whose black hair stood up in spiked clumps on his head, wore a chain around his neck with a gold skull emblem on it. Frankie had a small loop earring in one ear and skin so pale that for all Stewart knew he could have been a ghoul. Dirk had a pointed face that made him look like a weasel. All of them smoked.

With a slight kick of his black boot, Frankie came coasting toward Stewart, the slow clicking of his bike's freewheel ticking off the diminishing distance between them. Dirk and Judd glided toward him as well. Stewart pulled his backpack closer and backed against the deli window.

"Whatcha got in there?" Frankie asked, looking at his backpack.

"None of your business," Stewart replied, trying to keep his voice steady. "Nothing," he added quickly.

"Reeeeally," Frankie said, narrowing his eyes. "If you really had nothing, you would have said that in the first place. But you said it was none of our business, so you must have something. You wanna show us?"

Stewart looked from face to face. They were staring at him intently, like wolves eyeing cornered prey. He wished he could somehow melt back through the deli window, just lose his physical form for a moment and then rematerialize inside the shop. He thought about pushing back against the glass to see what might happen, but he didn't dare move.

"Let me rephrase the question," Frankie said. "You wanna show us what's in the pack, or you want us to do it ourselves?" He smiled a toothy grin. "I assure you, if you make us do it, it ain't gonna be much fun."

"Yeah, don't mess with the Rage," Judd said.

Dirk snickered.

Stewart was frozen with fear. Even if he had a good reply, his mouth was so dry he wouldn't have been able to get it out.

The bullies leaned forward slightly on their bikes, as though getting ready to spring. Stewart glanced around desperately. There were no adults in sight. He eyed the door to the deli. Frankie guessed what he was thinking and shot his bike forward, blocking the escape. Stewart gulped. Frankie to his right, Judd and Dirk to his left. No place to go but...straight?

Wait a second, Stewart thought. The street was a construction site. No cars! Did he dare?

Slowly the bullies rolled closer. Stewart knew he could get into huge trouble if he went into the site. Not only that, but it was dangerous and he could get hurt. But if he didn't try to escape now, he would soon be watching his coins ride off in the front pocket of Frankie's pants.

In a flash, Stewart sprang forward, darting between the front wheels of the bikes. The bullies, caught off guard, shouted in surprise. In two bounds, Stewart crossed the sidewalk and ducked under the yellow tape.

"Get him!" Frankie shouted.

Stewart heard the bikes crash to the sidewalk and the sound of footsteps in pursuit. Stewart realized almost immediately that they would be much faster than him. Since he couldn't outrun them, he'd have to evade.

Stewart heard them closing fast. He turned and dashed under the extended boom of a backhoe digger. He heard them curse as they had to slow down to stoop underneath. Stewart cut in a different direction and sprinted for a dump truck. The bullies charged after him. Just as they came up behind, Stewart reached the truck and slid under, forcing them to draw up short.

"He's a tricky little rat," Judd said between breaths.

"Split up!" Frankie yelled.

Without waiting for them to further organize their chase, Stewart darted out from under the other side of the truck and ran back toward the sidewalk, aiming for the deli door. He glanced back as he ran. To his horror, he saw that Judd had gone left, Dirk right, and Frankie was right behind him. Judd and Dirk were racing for the sidewalk to cut him off. Even if he did beat Frankie, he would just run right into the hands of Judd and Dirk. He was doomed.

As he hurdled a pile of asphalt clumps, Stewart spied the open storm drain, right next to the curb. He skidded to a stop at the opening just as Dirk and Judd ducked under the yellow tape and circled in front of him on the sidewalk to block his path. The hole was about six feet deep and had iron rungs, like a ladder, embedded into one wall. Judd and Dirk lunged forward to grab him. Without a second thought, Stewart scrambled down the rungs into the pit.

CHAPTER 3

Stewart crouched down on the gravel-covered bottom of the storm drain, out of reach, and looked up. The bullies, breathing heavily, stood circled around the drain opening, staring down at him. For a moment, no one moved. Then, as if on cue, the three of them each snorted up a loogie.

Stewart looked around desperately. A huge concrete water pipe about four feet in diameter connected with the drain in the wall opposite the rungs. Stewart leapt into the pipe just as three gobs of gooey spit rained down into the pit.

"Go get him," Stewart heard Frankie say.

"I'm not going down there," came Dirk's reply.

"What, you afraid of the rats?" Frankie asked.

At that, Stewart quickly looked down around his feet. But he didn't see any rats, just pebbles, sticks, and a flattened can.

"Why don't you go down there yourself?" Dirk shot back.

"Come on, twerp," Frankie called out. "We know you're down there. You've gotta come up at some point. Come up here now or you'll be sorry."

Stewart didn't know what they were planning, but it was clear they weren't going to come down. Although he was trapped, at least he and his coins were safe.

A clattering hunk of asphalt that caromed off the drain wall and came bouncing toward him made Stewart jump so hard that he banged his head on the top of the pipe. He barely managed to get out of the way of the projectile. He heard the Rage howl with laughter. They were throwing rocks down the drain! They could break his bones! What was wrong with them?

To say that Stewart hated the bullies was an understatement of giganticus, humongistic proportions. Ever since Stewart had moved to Harrison City and started at Oak Hill, they had made his life miserable. At recess, they had tormented him incessantly until he was forced to spend every day sitting near gray-haired Old Miss Wupplemeyer, the playground monitor. Stewart was convinced that she was almost blind, as she never seemed to notice problems more than twenty feet away. So Stewart sat by himself, every day, unable to make friends.

And because he had no friends, Stewart was forced to walk home alone, always at the mercy of the Rage. Within days of starting school, his walks had become panicked flights. Every day, those brick-brained brutes devised some new torture for him. The day before, they had caught him in the neighborhood and threatened to make him eat a dried dog turd. And his mom wasn't too happy when he got home with another knee tear, thanks to Frankie's parting shove. Stewart was going to tell her what happened, but if he did, his mom would be sure to call the school, the Rage would know he had told, and that would only make things worse.

Stewart had devised a plan that he felt certain would gain him not just a friend, but also an ally against the bullies. Two weeks before, Stewart had witnessed the most amazing scene at recess. From where Stewart had sat in his usual spot against the school wall near Old Miss Wupplemeyer, he had watched as the bullies walked up to Josh Johnson, who was in Stewart's class, and gave him a shove. Although Stewart was too far away to hear, Josh said something to the bullies. Dirk shoved him, and Josh said something again. Stewart was sure the confrontation was going to escalate into something very unpleasant for Josh, but after a few tense moments, the bullies simply turned and walked away. It was incredible: Josh was one of the smallest boys in the class and yet what he said had driven the bullies away.

So Stewart decided to bring his coins to school to show Josh. He figured that if he could impress Josh with his valuable old coins and become friends, Josh would share the secret words that drove the bullies away. But Josh had thought the coins were fake. Stewart had tried to point out that the wear and patina on the coins—the darkened copper, the dull nickel, the slightly tarnished silver—while not a guarantee of age certainly pointed to their authenticity. But Josh, for some reason, had closed his mind to the evidence. And now Stewart and his coins were trapped in a storm sewer.

A rattling of ricocheting rocks forced Stewart to retreat farther into the pipe. The last thing he needed was a broken arm. He sat watching, a safe distance from the drain, when all of a sudden a large cup of soda hit the bottom, splattering in all directions.

"That was awesome!" Judd yelled as Dirk and Frankie shrieked with laughter.

"Whaddaya think of that?" Frankie called down into the drain. "And guess what? There's a whole garbage can up here filled with all kinds of crap bombs. Come up now or prepare to be bombarded into oblivion."

Stewart thought about all the stuff that typically inhabited garbage cans—grease-stained takeout plates covered with leftover blobs of ketchup and mustard, bags of poop from people cleaning up after their dogs, loads of unidentifiable stinky and squishy objects. But there was no way he was giving up his coins. He pictured the construction site, with all the backhoes and jackhammers, and was struck by a sudden realization. The entire width of Ricrac Road had been cordoned off, so both sides must be under construction. Maybe there was an open drain on the other side of the street that he could crawl up through and then sneak away. The pipe he was in should lead to a main pipe in the middle of the street, from where he should be able to find another pipe to a drain on the other side.

As quietly as he could so the Rage wouldn't figure out what he was up to, Stewart crept through the drainpipe. The air grew damp and cool the farther he walked. He had only gone about twenty feet when he heard a concussive smack behind him as a big blob of gross and gooey garbage hit the pit bottom and splattered.

Stewart was glad he had moved farther into the pipe as the splash zone was fairly wide.

After going another thirty feet or so, Stewart spied a faint light shining into the pipe. He came to a cylindrical shaft that extended up to a wide metal disk with eight small round holes, the source of the light. Stewart examined it for a moment before realizing that he was looking up at the underside of a manhole cover.

A short distance farther, Stewart came to a junction where five pipes, including the one he was in, came together. All of them were illuminated by a hazy light, undoubtedly from manhole covers, and seemed to extend without end into the gloom.

What in the world? He had certainly gone farther than the distance to the other side of the street. And the pipe he was in hadn't curved; he should be far beyond the other side of the street at this point, maybe even to the next block. But that didn't make sense. Where was the main pipe?

Stewart looked back the way he had come. The drain was no longer visible. And all the other pipes looked the same. Stewart realized that he could easily get lost. He should mark the pipe that led back to the drain.

He looked around for a stick or can, but the pipe bottoms were fairly clean. He scraped at the pipe with the toe of his shoe, but the rubber didn't leave a visible mark on the concrete. Stewart thought for a moment more, then took off his backpack and put it in the pipe that led to the drain. He stepped away but then stopped. There was no way he was going to leave his coins behind. But then again, who would take them? If the Rage had wanted to come after him, they would have done so already. And he wouldn't be gone long. The coins would be safe.

Leaving his backpack in the pipe opening, Stewart entered the pipe that he guessed might lead to the other side of Ricrac Road, still puzzling over the strange pipe arrangement. After walking a good distance, he came to another junction of five pipes.

How can this be? he wondered. Storm sewer pipes followed streets; these pipes appeared to run at random. He stood in the middle of the junction, turning in a slow circle, looking down each pipe, hoping to spy a bright shaft of light coming from above, an indication of a way out. But they were all gloomy, illuminated by the same hazy light.

This is hopeless, he thought. The pipe layout made no sense, and anyway there appeared to be no way out. Better just to wait for the Rage to leave. Then he could just sneak out of the drain and go home. He'd get in trouble for being late, but at least he'd still have his coins.

Stewart headed back to the first junction to get his pack and return to the drain. But when he reached the junction, he stopped in shock. His pack was gone! One of the bullies must have come after him and stolen it! Then Stewart realized that there were six pipes forming the junction, not five; he was at the wrong junction. He must have gotten confused at the prior junction and taken the wrong pipe. He sighed in relief and walked back. He didn't know which pipe led back to the first junction, but there were only five of them. He would just have to follow each one until he found his pack.

Walking as quickly as he could, he followed three of the remaining four pipes. Each led to a junction, but no backpack. He practically ran down the last pipe, knowing that his pack would be there. But when he got to the junction, he skidded to a stop and stared. There were four pipes, not five, and no pack.

How could he have gotten lost? Stewart wondered. It made no sense! Stewart tried to calm his racing heart by taking deep breaths. Don't panic, he told himself. There had to be a way to find the drain.

He closed his eyes to think and immediately realized the answer. He could listen. The bullies certainly hadn't given up already, and they'd still be making taunts and hurling garbage into the drain.

Stewart listened, but heard nothing. The pipes were eerily quiet. Now and then he thought he detected some kind of hum or vibration coming from above, but nothing distinct. All the sounds were muffled, as though he had cotton in his ears. He waited and waited but still didn't hear anything. And his rumbling stomach told him that it was getting close to dinnertime.

Stewart was stumped. Had he really wandered so far from the construction site that the bullies were no longer audible? Unlikely, but possible. But if he didn't find his way back to the drain, he'd have to call for help. They'd have to pry off a manhole cover to get him out. There'd be police, and the fire department, and probably news vans too. He'd be on TV, with dramatic footage of him being hoisted out in a rescue basket. The video clip would hit the Internet and go viral. Everyone would see it and for the rest of his life he'd be known as "Sewer Boy."

Stewart started exploring the pipes, trying to find a way out. After wandering for what felt like hours, he finally took a pipe that made him whoop in relief. At the end of the pipe was a very faint light. At last, an exit! It wasn't the drain where he'd entered, but by now the Rage were probably long gone. He'd just find his way back to the construction site, scramble down and get his pack, and be on his way home. He might get in trouble for being late, but Stewart was so relieved that he didn't care.

As Stewart approached the end of the pipe, he saw that a dense cluster of leafy branches covered the opening. As he got closer, he slowed down. The leaves growing on the branches were slender, elongated green ovals, but they ended in bright orange points. Orange? He reached out and touched one carefully in case it was a sharp thorn. It was soft, just like the rest of the leaf. He pushed his way through the branches. And what he saw on the other side made him catch his breath.

CHAPTER 4

Stewart stepped out of the pipe into a forest of bushes and trees growing on the side of a hill. The vegetation was unlike anything he had ever seen. The bushes growing directly in front of the pipe opening had grown in a zigzag shape. The leaf ends were such a bright orange that, in the light, they appeared to be on fire. Smaller bushes growing among the zigzag bushes had a pumpkin shape, round spheres of yellow and green leaves with a sprig of trunk, like a stem, sticking out the top. The surrounding trees had twisted trunks with wide canopies of greenish-blue leaves, some such an intense blue that they looked purple. Twisted vines snaked along the ground, brown ropy shafts covered in what appeared to be patches of pink lichen.

Stewart reached out and carefully touched the leaf of a tree. It felt just like any other leaf. He had almost expected it to be fake. He turned it over. The leaf had intricate veins the color of gold. He let go of the leaf and looked around. What was this place? Had he emerged from the pipe into some strange part of Cloverleaf Park, which bordered his neighborhood?

He heard a gentle whooshing sound, like cars passing by somewhere off in the distance. The park was a big place, and he had not yet explored all of it. And a busy road did encircle the park. He decided to climb the hill to get his bearings.

He trudged to the top, picking his way through the strange and colorful plants, and emerged from the forest to a sight that made him stop short. Before him lay a long, grassy slope, darker green than any field he had ever before seen, dotted with flowers of pink and purple and bushes in searing reds, brilliant yellows, and bright oranges. The trees that bordered the edges of the field were massive, with wide trunks and sweeping limbs covered with leaves in colors that spanned the spectrum. Birds—the kind he would expect to find in a jungle—filled the air, while butterflies flitted and bees buzzed from flower to flower. In the distance, beyond swaths of forest, stood a range of mountains, their emerald-green lower slopes giving way to gray and brown rock shoulders before ending in peaks frosted with caps of snow.

What had sounded like a steady flow of cars turned out to be a gently gurgling river, the sparkling water a deep sapphire blue, running at the bottom of the grassy slope. Stewart could not see a single building, bridge, car, truck, bus, airplane, sidewalk, or street. Worse, he could not see a single person.

A loud crashing and crackling of branches coming from a nearby grove of scrub made him jump. Moments later, an enormous deer appeared, twice the size of any deer he had ever seen. It stood over ten feet high, its brown, glossy coat covering front shoulders and hindquarters rippling with muscles. A great rack of antlers graced its head. The deer turned and fixed its gaze on Stewart. He stood, unable to move, staring back at the creature. Then the deer turned and walked away at an unhurried pace, following the edge of the grove before disappearing from sight.

Stewart stood, half in shock. This place was wrong. It didn't make sense. He had to get home.

He turned and ran down the slope to the pipe, jumping over scrub, dodging trees, and pushing through bushes. He would get back into the pipe, get far away from this bizarro-land, and find his way home. It didn't matter how long it took, or if he got grounded for a year.

He saw the zigzag and pumpkin-like bushes as he flew past them, his momentum carrying him farther down the slope until he managed to skid to a stop. He ran back up the hill and practically dove into the branches that covered the pipe opening. He crashed through the bushes.

And landed on the ground behind them.

CHAPTER 5

Stewart lay on the dirt in the cluster of bushes for a moment, confused. He looked to each side, but there was no pipe. Where had it gone? He got up and pushed his way back out through the branches. The grove was the same. Same bushes, same trees, same vines snaking over the ground. He carefully parted the branches again. No pipe.

He felt a wave of panic. Large concrete drainpipes didn't just disappear! He took deep breaths, trying to slow his racing heart. There had to be some explanation for this. He must have gotten confused. The plants were so colorful; maybe he was in fact in the wrong grove. Maybe he had run down the hill so fast that he had gone off course. That had to be it.

He traversed the hillside, looking for the right zigzag bushes. Twice he found some, but they weren't concealing the pipe. Either he was lost, or the pipe had somehow disappeared. But it couldn't have! He must have gotten lost. That was the only explanation. No matter, he decided. With the dim light and all the junctions, he could easily get lost again if he tried to go back through the pipe. He'd just have to find another way back. He couldn't have gone that far through the pipes anyway, so he must still be near Harrison City. And there had to be someone around who could direct him home.

He climbed the hill and stopped for a moment at the top to study the expanse around him. He had never seen flowers and trees and bushes of such colors. And all the birds, bees, and butterflies—his neighborhood had the usual bird or bug here and there, but not the number and variety he saw now. Strange trees, colorful plants...

Then the answer hit him: he was in the Harrison City Botanical Garden! His class at Oak Hill was planning a field trip to visit, and his teacher had talked about all the strange and wonderful plants brought in from around the world. That had to be it! There was no other logical explanation. And the Botanical Garden would have birds and bugs from the plants' original habitats as well, to create a natural environment. That explained all the birds and insects. He laughed with relief.

Unable to spot anyone from his vantage point, he decided to head down to the river. Perhaps he would run into someone fishing or boating. If anything, Stewart knew that a person lost in the wilderness should follow a river downstream, as all rivers eventually lead to a town or city. The river must lead to Harrison City.

He started off down the grassy slope. He would be home in no time, he was certain. It didn't matter that he couldn't see any roads or buildings; he'd once been in a zoo that was so well-designed with trees and rocks and expanses of grass for the animals that he had felt like he was in the middle of the Serengeti. And the mountains...he must have dozed off when he and his mom followed the moving van from their old home to Harrison City. That's why he hadn't noticed them before.

As he walked, his feet swishing through the grass, he heard a faint snapping sound. He made his way quickly in the direction of the sound, cutting across the field toward a thick circular hedge of bushes about six feet high that very much looked like small, cylindrical pine trees. However, instead of being green, the needles were pink where they grew from the branch and intensified in color until they ended in deep scarlet tips. The snapping sound came from within the ring of bushes.

Stewart tried to see through the branches but the needles were too dense. He crouched down into the grass and peered underneath the lowermost branches. He saw someone's shoes, which occasionally rose up onto tiptoe. The shoes, however, were the strangest he'd ever seen; they were made of a thick coarse cloth, beige in color, and were tied around the ankles with what looked like lengths of vine.

"Hello?" Stewart called out.

Stewart heard a gasp and the snapping sound immediately stopped. For a moment, there was only silence. Then Stewart saw a face, a girl, looking back at him.

The girl let out a deep breath. "You startled me!" she said. "You know that's forbidden out here!" She studied his face for a moment. "Wait a second, do I know you?"

"I'm Stewart. I just moved here."

"You've just arrived?" the girl asked. "Hold on, let me come out of here."

A moment later, she emerged from the bushes, pushing through a place where the branches thinned. She was about his height, maybe a little shorter, and she wore a crude shirt and pants crafted of the same coarse beige cloth as her shoes. Her pants, like her shoes, were tied with a vine. Her skin was very fair, almost pure white.

The girl held a strange basket, a narrow oval of tightly woven reeds about six inches deep. Attached to the top edge on one side was a flap of the coarse cloth and to each end of the basket a longer length of the cloth that served as a strap. The basket contained what appeared to be small berries, but nothing like Stewart had seen before in his life. Each berry was in the shape of a *c*, colored in twisting bands of red and blue. Stewart realized that the snapping was the sound of the girl picking berries.

"I'm Cora," she said. She studied his clothes for a moment before returning to his gaze with a wide smile.

"What *is* this place?" Stewart asked, gesturing to the landscape around them.

"It's very interesting, isn't it," she said slowly. She seemed to be choosing her words carefully.

"You got that right," he said, laughing, happy that he had found someone and that he wasn't the only one who found the place to be so strange. "Is this the Botanical Garden?"

"Yes, it is," she said. "The Botanical Garden."

"I knew it!" Stewart said, laughing. "For a minute, I thought I was on the other side of the planet. They really did a good job making this place look like the middle of nowhere."

"How did you get here?" she asked.

"Through a drainpipe, up there on the hill," he said, pointing.

"And where do you live?" she asked.

"Harrison City!" he said, thinking that was a funny question. "Where else?"

"Me too," she said. Cora looked past him and scanned the area, her face briefly taking on an expression of concern. "What do you say we head back there now?"

"Let's go," he said.

Cora flipped the cloth flap over the basket opening, slung it over her shoulder, and they started walking in the direction of the river.

"Come on," she said, breaking into a jog.

Stewart increased his pace. "What's the rush?" he asked.

"It's getting late," she said, "and I need to get back. Hope you don't mind a little exercise."

"No, not at all," Stewart said. He actually liked the sound their feet made as they tromped through the grass and the slightly rubbery feel of the thick green blades.

Stewart wanted to ask Cora about her clothes. He had never met anyone who dressed like that. But then he realized that she might get offended. She was helping him, after all.

As they ran, he noticed that she kept glancing back over her shoulder. Then, without warning, she turned and pulled him behind a bush, stopped, and peered back in the direction they had come. He looked at her quizzically.

"Did I show you these?" she asked quickly, opening the basket.

"What are those things?" Stewart asked.

"Swirl berries," Cora said. "Here, have some."

Stewart hesitated; he had never seen anything like them before and knew the dangers of eating wild berries. But then Cora took a handful and popped them into her mouth, so Stewart plucked one out and tasted it. The berry tasted like a mix of orange juice and vanilla ice cream.

"Good, huh?" she asked.

"They're delicious," Stewart said, taking a handful. "But are you allowed to pick them?" He had never heard of a botanical garden where people could pick the fruit of the plants.

She glanced back up the slope, then pulled his arm and started off running again.

"Of course we can pick them," she said. "That's one of the things we can do in the..." Her face turned red. "What did you call this place again?"

"The Botanical Garden," Stewart said.

"Right," Cora said, laughing nervously. "I don't know how I forgot that. I guess I just come here so much that I don't think of the name."

The river ahead was wide and smooth, with occasional ripples that glittered golden in the late afternoon light. When they reached the river, they slowed to a walk. Stewart was breathing heavily, but Cora didn't seem winded in the least. She paused a moment to look behind them and scan the area, then led Stewart along the bank toward a huge tree. The tree grew right along the bank and had a wide canopy that extended far out over the river.

"What are you looking for?" Stewart asked.

"Nothing," she said. "Just taking in the sight. It's so beautiful here."

Stewart didn't know if he should believe her, but decided to let it go. All he wanted to do was get home.

The branches of the tree were covered with green leaves and maroon blossoms. Like the branches of a willow tree, they sprang out from the trunk in all directions and then dropped straight down to touch the grass, the bank, and the surface of the water. The overlapping leaves and blossoms created a dense curtain of green and red. Cora parted the branches and motioned for Stewart to pass through the opening she had created. As he entered, she looked back the way they had come, then slipped in behind him.

Stewart found himself standing inside a dome of branches that sheltered a section of the bank and part of the river, creating a hidden cove. A boat, unlike any that Stewart had ever seen, rested halfway up on shore. Wider than a canoe but narrower than a rowboat, the boat was formed from a hollowed-out tree trunk to which outriggers of long slender logs had been attached on both sides. The interior contained two seats made from simple wooden planks. Two long oars rested in wooden oarlocks, the blades tucked into the boat near the stern. The boat's exterior was coated with what looked like a reddish-brown tar or resin.

"Let me get it out into the water and then we'll get in," she said.

"That's yours?" Stewart asked. It was the coolest boat he had ever seen.

"I just use it when I need it," Cora said. She unslung the basket, put it in the bottom of the boat, and grabbed the bow to push it back into the water. "It doesn't really belong—"

From a distance came a growling sound, followed by a series of grunts, a sound that made the hairs on Stewart's neck stand up. Cora froze, then crouched down. The sounds were deep and guttural, and sounded to Stewart like the kind that came from a mouth lined with long, sharp teeth. The sounds came again, only louder. Stewart realized, to his growing horror, that whatever was making those sounds was approaching the curtain of branches.

CHAPTER 6

Cora motioned with her hand for Stewart to get down and brought her finger to her lips. They heard a rustle of grass just on the other side of the branches and more growling. Stewart pressed himself as low to the ground as he could. He had no idea what was out there, but he knew with certainty that he didn't want to meet it.

There were more rustling sounds, then silence, then the sound of something slowly heading away from the river. Stewart and Cora remained motionless until whatever it was could no longer be heard. Then Cora stood up and carefully pushed the boat into the water.

"Get in," she whispered.

Stewart climbed into the boat and took the seat closest to the stern. Cora put one foot in and shoved off the bank with the other. Stewart ducked as the boat brushed through the branches and out into the river. Cora stepped past him, sat down in the other seat, lowered the oar blades into the water, and started quickly rowing the boat upstream against the current. After a while, Cora slowed the pace of her strokes.

"What was that?" Stewart asked.

Cora didn't immediately answer. After a moment, she said, "Those were guard dogs."

That explained all the running and her hiding behind the bush and looking over her shoulder! She was a thief! Stewart's eyes narrowed.

"You're not supposed to be picking berries, are you?" He had no interest in being chased by dogs, especially ones that sounded like rabid werewolves, or getting caught stealing fruit.

Cora gave him a sheepish grin. "You're right. I'm not supposed to pick the berries. But don't worry, they won't catch us. I've escaped from them countless times. Trust me."

Stewart sat back, a little uneasy and slightly annoyed that Cora was putting him at risk of getting busted for stealing. He was glad he left his backpack behind; he didn't want his coins anywhere near this girl. But she was leading him back to the city, so there really was nothing he could do but just go along with it. If they did get caught, he certainly would explain that he had nothing to do with the berry picking. *He* wasn't the one always sneaking in there. He checked his hands for swirl berry juice just in case anyone examined them for evidence. Seeing one stain, he quickly licked his finger and wiped it on his pants.

Cora worked the oars easily, keeping the boat in the center of the river and moving at a constant speed. Stewart was surprised at her strength. She was small but didn't seem to tire. As they continued up the meandering river, Stewart scanned the horizon for some sign of Harrison City. He was sure that at any moment houses would appear, or a road, or a canoe rental shop, or at least someone jogging along a path or sitting on a bench, reading. But he saw no sign of the city.

"Is the city much farther?" Stewart asked.

"It's still a little ways off, but don't worry, we'll get there," Cora said.

Stewart peered around eagerly. At any moment, he was certain something would come into view that would allow him to see how this strange place connected to the familiar. They rounded a bend, and a gap in the trees lining the bank provided the most unexpected sight.

In the middle of a wide, grassy plain stood a large circular wall at least a hundred feet high, constructed of drab gray stones that contrasted sharply with the colorful foliage surrounding it. The entire structure lacked windows or features of any kind save for a small entrance gate, sealed off by wooden doors, which occupied an arch in the wall facing the river. The place looked gloomy and foreboding.

"What is that?" Stewart asked as he dropped back to his seat. "It looks like some kind of prison."

"You're right," Cora said. "It's a prison. And we actually have to make a quick stop there. I, um, I have to drop off these berries, for a friend's mom."

"Your friend's mom is in prison?" Stewart asked. He caught glimpses of the wall between the tree trunks. "What'd she do?"

"I'm not sure," Cora said. "We don't really talk about it."

At a section of riverbank covered with dense bushes, Cora pulled on one oar, pushed on the other, and the bow of the boat spun in toward the shore. She gave one last hard pull and the boat slid partway up the bank and came to a stop. She lifted the oars out of the oarlocks and tucked them inside the boat. They both got out, and Cora pulled the boat out of the water and dragged it into the bushes, completely obscuring it with the branches. She emerged carrying the swirl berry basket. She took Stewart's arm and led him to the top of the bank, in sight of the wall.

"Now listen to me carefully," Cora said, her face stern and serious. "Visiting hours for the prison are almost over, so we've got to get inside quickly. Just stay low and follow me."

As Stewart stood there, staring at the wall, it dawned on him that something didn't look right about the prison. There were no electrical wires leading to the building, no lights on the wall, no other fencing or wire. As a matter of fact, there were no roads that led to the prison or to the front entrance gate.

Stewart looked in all directions but could see no sign of civilization. They had traveled a good distance up the river but yet there was no trace, anywhere, of Harrison City. He realized, suddenly, that not only was he still far from home, but Cora wasn't telling him the truth.

"Hold on a second," Stewart said, pulling his arm from her grasp. "I'm not going in there."

"Visiting hours are almost over," Cora repeated.

"That's not a prison," Stewart said.

"It is so," insisted Cora. "Are you calling me a liar? You're so mean." She suddenly looked like she was going to cry.

For a moment Stewart felt guilty; he didn't mean to hurt her feelings. But he saw that she was studying his face. She wasn't hurt; she was faking it. She was obviously trying to trick him.

"Tell me where Harrison City is," Stewart demanded.

Her sad expression vanished instantly. "I'll explain once we get inside," Cora said.

"Explain?" Stewart asked. "What explanation could there be for a whole city disappearing?"

"Please, Stewart, you have to trust me," Cora said. "Those, um, dogs we ran into are headed this way and we'll get into huge trouble if they catch us."

"What, you're afraid of the dogs? I'd rather get chased by some angry hounds than go into that place," Stewart said, pointing at the massive stone wall.

"Okay, Stewart, here's the truth," Cora said, her voice firm. "Those creatures we encountered near the boat weren't dogs, this isn't the Botanical Garden, and that's not a prison. I know where Harrison City is, and I'll tell you, but it is too hard to explain here and now. Please," she said, growing visibly nervous and looking all around, "we can't stay here any longer."

"If they weren't dogs, what were they?" Stewart asked.

"We call them Venators," Cora said.

"Venators?"

"It means 'hunter.' They're very tall, very thin, extremely scary, and totally relentless. That's a Venator."

Stewart stared at Cora, not sure what to make of what she was saying. Was she joking? But her expression was serious.

"Well, then, what is that place?" Stewart asked, pointing at the wall.

"That's where I live, where we all live," Cora said.

A feeling of panic welled up inside Stewart. He turned in all directions, looking for some sign of home.

"Stewart!" Cora said sharply.

Stewart stopped and faced her.

"I know this whole place is very strange. And you don't understand what is going on. But you have to trust me. We have to go now," she said. "Darkness is coming and you don't want to be outside after dark."

"But what is this place?" Stewart asked, almost shouting. "That wall, this grass, the plants, the leaves—"

"Keep your voice down!" Cora hissed. "Stewart, we have to get inside the wall *now!*"

"Are you crazy?" Stewart asked, staring at the wall. "I'm not going in there. I have to get back to Harrison City. I have to get home."

"Stewart," Cora said gently, but firmly. "Do you see the sun?"

What a crazy question, Stewart thought. It was right... Stewart scanned the cloudless sky, but could not see the sun. He looked at how the shadows lay and then up in the sky to where the sun should be. One spot in the sky was brighter, but he could still detect the unbroken blue of the sky in the brightness. He looked again at the shadows. They were faint and somewhat indistinct. Stewart felt as though they were under a dome of opaque blue glass, ringed by the mountains, with a light shining in from the other side of the glass. He started to shake with fear. How could the sun have disappeared?

"Stewart, please," Cora said. "You have to trust me; I'll explain everything once we're inside. But it's not safe to be out here any longer. Those Venators who almost found us are headed our way. There is no other place for you to go." She stared at a point in the distance and then gasped. "Oh no," she said. "Here they come."

Stewart looked in the direction of her stare. Across the field, walking at a brisk pace at the edge of the trees, were three figures. The figures resembled humans but were nearly double the size of the tallest adult he had ever seen, with thin, sinewy bodies. They wore no clothes except for dirty cloths around their waists. Their skin was pasty yellow and their heads, with gaunt faces and matted wisps of gray hair, appeared skeletal. Their faces were twisted into snarls and their eyes were piercing and determined, as though hunting prey.

CHAPTER 7

Cora grabbed Stewart by the front of his shirt, yanked him down low, and dragged him behind the nearest bush.

"Now you listen to me and listen good," she said, her breathing becoming more rapid. "I'm your Finder, so it is my responsibility to get you safely inside. But I'm not going to risk my own skin over you. You can either come with me or take your chances with the Venators. What's it going to be?"

Stewart was so frightened that he couldn't speak. He nodded vigorously.

"Good," she said. "You see those trees growing at the base of the wall?"

Stewart looked to where she was pointing. At different places around the wall grew clusters of trees and bushes. Stewart wasn't sure which cluster she was pointing to, but he nodded anyway.

"That's where we're headed. It's the closest port."

"Not those doors?" he managed to croak, indicating the entrance gate.

"No, we rarely open them." She raised herself up until she could see just over the top of the bush. "The Venators are still a good distance away and haven't seen us. Stay low and follow me. Do not raise your head, and do not make a sound."

Cora took off running. Stewart followed, doing his best to keep up. They dashed to the nearest bush and crouched down. Cora pointed to another bush, and they ran as fast as they could toward it and dropped down behind it. Cora raised her head, looked around, then took off again.

When they were about halfway to the wall, Stewart heard a cry, deep and guttural.

"They've spotted us!" Cora shouted. "Just run, Stewart, run! And don't look back!"

Racing at top speed, they ran across the field, making a beeline for the cluster of trees and bushes. When they reached the dense thicket, they drew up short, breathing heavily. The perimeter of the growth was guarded by pricker bushes, long straight stalks covered with inch-long thorns. Cora adjusted the basket slung on her back before reaching out and carefully grabbing one of the stalks.

"Careful," she said. "These are scritchy bushes. The prickers are really sharp and will make your skin itch for an hour if you get scratched. The Venators hate them, so we plant them around all the ports. Hurry now."

Cora slowly made her way past the branches and Stewart followed. It was tricky going, and he had to bend and twist to slip past the thorny stalks. But finally he was through and made it to the wall. About two feet off the ground was a circular wooden door. It looked like the porthole cover of a ship. In the center of the door, instead of a doorknob, was a large knot of rope.

Cora pulled on the rope knot and the door swung to one side, revealing a dark and narrow tunnel in the stone wall. The rope that was attached to the door extended inside.

"It's a tight fit, but that helps deter the Venators from coming in. Just pull yourself through with the rope."

They couldn't see outside the thicket, but they could hear the faint thumping of approaching footsteps.

"Go, quickly now," Cora said.

Stewart knelt down and peered in. The tunnel seemed to extend about fifteen feet. At the other end was a dimly lit space, the visible far wall made of stone. Stewart could see what looked like wooden crates stacked against the wall. The rope was anchored to a peg embedded in the wall.

Stewart extended his arms and shoved himself into the tunnel. He grabbed onto the rope and pulled. The feeling of being inside the tight-fitting stone tube was extremely disconcerting. He tried not to think about getting stuck and kept pulling. He finally tumbled out the other end, into a small room, and lay on the floor, breathing hard.

A moment later, Cora, pushing her basket ahead of her, exited more gracefully, using the rope to swing out and land on her feet. She pulled the rope tight and Stewart heard the door at the other end of the tunnel snap closed. Cora wrapped the slack of the rope around the anchor peg, securing the door.

"Are you okay?" Cora asked.

Stewart nodded. He slowly rose to his feet and dusted off his pants. Try as he might, he couldn't get the image of the three creatures or the memory of the sounds they made out of his mind.

"That happens all the time," Cora said. "The Venators always try to get us on the return. But no matter, we're safe now. Come on."

"Where are we going?" Stewart asked.

"To the Curia to see the Princeps," Cora said. "She's our leader and will explain everything."

Although Stewart's head was still spinning from all that had happened, at Cora's words he felt relieved. They were going to see someone in charge. His mom had always told him that if he ever got in serious trouble he should immediately seek out an adult to help. Stewart couldn't wait to find out the explanation for this place and especially how to get back home.

Cora led Stewart out of the room into what appeared to be a warehouse. The stone perimeter walls were lined with wooden shelves, which held crates filled with what appeared to be odd-looking fruits, roots, vegetables, and leaves. Children dressed similarly to Cora were cleaning and sorting on tables in the middle of the room, using cloths to wipe fruit or brush dirt from roots before putting them into crates. The interior of the warehouse was lit not by light bulbs but rather by open hatches in the roof, which was made of thatch and supported by stout beams. The wide open doors provided light as well. All of the children, Stewart noticed, were pale, some even more so than Cora.

"What is this place?" Stewart asked.

"This is our Food Store, where everybody gets their food," Cora said to Stewart, handing over her basket to one of the children. "I'm a Gatherer. My job is to bring whatever food I collect here and the Sorters put it into crates. It gets stored here or, if it is really fresh or perishable or we have more than we can eat immediately, we put it in the Cold Store."

The sight that greeted Stewart when Cora led him out of the Food Store made him stop short. The wall, at least a hundred feet high, encircled a city at least a mile across. The buildings were all small, mostly single-story structures constructed of the same drab stone as the wall, each topped by a thatched roof. Openings in the walls formed the windows and doors, which were covered with a curtain of the same coarse cloth as the children's clothing. The streets and alleys were either cobbled or dirt paths. No matter where he looked, he could not see a single electric light, phone or power wire, or anything made of glass or steel. It was as though he had stepped out into a medieval city.

The interior curve of the wall was broken at evenly spaced intervals by round stone towers that ran from the base to the very top. A vertical row of circular windows ran the full height of each tower, but beyond that the towers were featureless. Stewart couldn't figure out their purpose until he noticed people moving about the top of the wall. He looked more closely and saw stairs through the windows. The towers, he realized, enclosed stairways that led up to the top of the wall.

What struck Stewart most about the city was the dimness of the light. The high wall shrouded the city in a gloomy shadow. Stewart felt as though he were standing at the bottom of an enormous smokestack. And the air—in contrast with the warmth and fragrance outside the wall, the city felt cold and damp.

The only people in the streets were children, and Stewart couldn't believe how pale they all were. In the dim light, their skin was so white that they almost appeared to be glowing.

Stewart followed Cora down a wide avenue that led toward a large square building, at least three times the width of any building Stewart had seen so far. The wall of the building was dotted with small windows and in the center, in line with the avenue, was a set of double doors. A wispy column of smoke rose from a hole in the center of the roof.

"This is the Curia," Cora said when they finally reached the front doors.

Inside, they followed a wide hallway illuminated by torches set in sconces. They turned down another hallway and came to a door. Outside the door was a boy standing stiffly at attention.

"We need to see the Princeps," Cora said to the boy.

"She's in a Third Prophecy planning session and cannot be disturbed," the boy said.

"We have a Newcomer," Cora said, gesturing to Stewart.

The boy looked at Stewart, his eyes opening wide. "Wait here," he said. The boy opened the door and went into the room.

"He's a Defender," Cora explained to Stewart. "They defend the city and maintain order."

To Stewart, the wait felt like an eternity. On the other side of that door was salvation. He would finally talk to an adult and get this whole matter cleared up.

At last, the door opened fully, revealing a large room. In the center of the room was a stone pyre on which burned a wood-fueled fire, the smoke rising in lazy curls and exiting through a hole in the roof that had been lined with what appeared to be dried mud. On one side of the room was a sitting area consisting of a sofa of sorts—a wooden frame constructed of tree branches with the bark removed and lashed tightly together with vines with a cushion made of the same material as the children's clothing—as well as a half-dozen cushions lying on the floor. On the other side of the room was a large, rough-hewn table at which sat five people, four boys and a girl, as pale as all the other children. When Stewart and Cora entered the room, the children sitting around the table rose to their feet.

Stewart looked around the room, puzzled.

"Where's your leader?" he whispered to Cora, looking around for an adult.

"She's right there," she said.

Cora pointed to the girl at the table.

CHAPTER 8

Stewart felt his knees weaken and the sensation of the floor rising up to meet him. Cora quickly grabbed him under one shoulder and the Defender grabbed him under the other, and they led him to the sofa. He sat down onto the sofa's cushion, stuffed with what felt like straw. A boy handed Stewart a wooden cup of water, and he took a sip. The girl that Cora had indicated was the Princeps shooed everyone out of the room except for Cora and one of the boys who had been sitting at the table, a tall boy with curly red hair and strong arms.

The Princeps approached slowly and took a seat on one of the cushions on the floor. Cora and the other boy sat on a cushion on either side of the Princeps. For a long time, no one spoke, the only sound the crackling of the fire.

"How are you feeling?" the Princeps finally asked.

"Better, I think," Stewart said. He took another sip of water, trying to clear the lightness from his head.

"Good," she said. "My name is Evelyn, and I am the Princeps of the city. This is Lester, the Chief Defender," she said, pointing to the boy. "You've already met Cora. And what is your name?"

"Stewart," he said.

"Stewart," the Princeps said with a slight smile. "I like that name. Tell me, Stewart, where are you from?"

"Harrison City," he answered.

"And what's it like there?" she asked.

Stewart told about his school and his house and his gaming console and what he did after school and the things he liked to watch on TV.

"What year is it?" she asked.

Stewart hesitated. That was a strange question. But he told them the year. When he did, the Princeps brought one hand to her chest and, for a moment, got a faraway look in her eyes.

"And how did you get here?" she asked, refocusing on him.

Stewart explained about being chased down the drain by the bullies, getting lost in the pipes, and popping out on the side of the hill by the river. When he finished, she nodded slowly.

"Stewart," she said, "what I'm about to tell you is going to sound very strange. However, before I tell you, you should know that every single child in this city has the same story as you. You are no different than anyone else here, including me.

"You are in a land we call Bitopia. There are fields and forests, lakes and rivers, all ringed by a mountain range. This is the only city in Bitopia, and all the citizens are children. No one actually knows where Bitopia is, but we are fairly confident that we are no longer on the planet Earth."

Stewart felt a shock of fear at those words and fought to keep control of his breathing.

"We live within this high wall as protection from the Venators, who wander the land. We don't know much about them—what they do or why they are here.

Their only purpose seems to be to hunt us down. Occasionally they lay siege to the city. However, they have never been able to breach the wall, and eventually they go away. Only the Gatherers, who collect food and other supplies, have to venture out."

That explains the paleness of everyone's skin, Stewart realized. All the citizens live in perpetual shadow.

"Every citizen in the city," the Princeps continued, "arrived here the same way as you. Each citizen hid from tormentors and then, when he or she thought the danger had passed, emerged from hiding and found him or herself in this land.

"In my case, I was at a boarding school, and the girls there just hated me. One night after dinner, as we were returning to our rooms from the dining hall, I overheard them talking about forcing the ends of my hair into my inkwell. So I ran and hid in a closet. When I thought it was safe to come out, I found myself in a nearby forest." The Princeps looked at Lester.

"I was trying to escape some boys at summer camp," Lester said, "and hid underwater in a swimming hole, breathing through a reed. When I came up, I found myself in the river."

"I ducked behind a trash barrel in my neighborhood in New York, trying to escape from Ugly Velma and her Gang of Five," Cora said. "She was a terror, and I hated her. But when I stepped out, I found myself in a grove of fober trees."

"You see, Stewart," the Princeps said, "every citizen of this city has a similar story."

Stewart nodded in understanding. Somehow his trying to escape the bullies had caused him to wind up in this place.

"But why don't you go home?" Stewart asked.

"We don't know how," the Princeps said. "We've tried to get beyond the mountains, but the one expedition that managed to reach the top of one only saw more frozen and icy mountains as far as the eye could see."

"What happened to the closet door in the field that brought you here?" Stewart asked.

"The portals that bring us here are one-way. They disappear after they've been used. Your drainpipe, for example. If you went back to where it brought you, you would not find it."

Stewart thought back to when he ascended the hill and then came back down and couldn't find the pipe. He hadn't gone off track; the pipe had in fact disappeared.

"I know," she said, seeing the expression on Stewart's face. "This can be very hard to accept."

"There has to be a way back home," he said.

"We've tried," she said. "All of us want to go home. But we can't get out."

"So how long have you been here?" Stewart asked.

The Princeps took a deep breath. "I got here in 1903," she said.

"It was 1950 when I arrived," Lester said.

"1924," Cora volunteered.

"Wait," Stewart said, starting to shake slightly. "Princeps Evelyn, that would make you over one hundred years old."

"We don't age here," the Princeps said. "The days pass but we don't change. It is one of the many mysteries of Bitopia."

Stewart took a deep breath, trying to slow his racing heart. He was no longer on Earth. Time passed, but no one aged. The Princeps was over a hundred years old but still a girl. Everyone lived in the city shrouded in shadow. And the only thing protecting them from the Venators was the wall.

"How long have people been here?" Stewart asked.

"I'm actually the oldest person here," the Princeps said. "That's what 'Princeps' means: 'first citizen.' When I arrived the city had already been built. The city had been occupied at some point in the past, but I found it empty."

"What happened to everyone?" Stewart asked, his hope rising. "Did they somehow get home?"

The Princeps looked at Lester.

"He's going to find out eventually," Lester said to the Princeps. "And we all agreed it is better to answer the questions of the Newcomers to maintain their trust rather than withhold information."

The Princeps nodded. "A few years after I arrived," she said, "and as the population of the city began to swell and we started using more and more of the empty houses, we noticed that one small building in the

47

center of the city was made completely of stone and had no windows or doors. The outline of a door was visible, but it had been filled in with stone. We slowly chipped away at the mortar and eventually broke through. Inside we found a book, the Comlat.

"The book was written by the prior occupants of the city, who we call our Forebears, and contains all their knowledge about the land and how to live off it. It is from the Comlat that we know where to find fruits and vegetables, how to make our clothing, how to work with wood and make mortar for the wall. It is our most precious possession. Without it we wouldn't survive.

"The Comlat contains a passage that we call the Third Prophecy because it describes a third and final battle between the Forebears and the Venators. In the battle, the Venators entered the city and the citizens were defeated."

"Why do you call it a prophecy?" Stewart asked.

"Because the Forebears predicted their own defeat," the Princeps said.

"Theirs and ours," Lester added.

The Princeps quickly raised her hand. "The future is not guaranteed," she said to Lester. Apparently it was a point on which the Princeps and Lester didn't agree.

"The Comlat describes three battles," the Princeps continued, "two in which the Venators are repelled, the third in which they are victorious. So far since we've been here, the Venators have attacked the city twice, both times exactly as described in the Comlat. If history is any guide, then according to the Prophecy, when the Venators attack again, they will enter the city and defeat us."

Stewart thought about the generation of children that occupied the city. A whole teeming city, wiped out in one battle. Their knowledge written in a book, their history this city's future. And Stewart trapped here, with no way home. He would be here and never age until a final battle with the Venators.

"No," Stewart said. "I can't accept this. All of this. It's not right."

"I know," the Princeps said. "We all felt the same way when we first arrived. Assimilation can be very hard. But that's okay, Stewart, it was the same for all of us. In time, you'll accept the city as your home. And you should know that we are quite happy here. We have the protection of the wall, and the lands around provide ample food, plants from which we make clothes, wood for making other necessities, and stones to build new houses and the wall higher."

"But this can't be real," Stewart said, his voice rising. "I mean, not on Earth?"

The Princeps raised her hand. "Let's stop talking about this now," she said. "You must be tired and hungry, and a good night's sleep will help. We'll show you to your quarters. As Cora is your Finder, you'll be her charge for the time being."

"But—" Stewart started to protest.

"In the morning," the Princeps said. "Trust me, it will be better to talk more then."

Not having any other choice, Stewart rose and followed the Princeps through the building to a small room that contained a cot. A lit torch hung in a sconce on the wall, directly under which was a bucket of sand. The Princeps instructed Stewart to plunge the torch into the sand to extinguish it when he was ready to go to sleep. Cora would meet him in the morning to begin his Orientation. As she turned to go, a boy arrived with a wooden tray of food, a large wooden vessel of water, and a cup and set it on the floor.

Stewart was famished, so he sat down next to the tray. He poured himself a cup of water and downed it, then refilled it and took two more gulps. The tray contained some swirl berries as well as an assortment of globes, tubes, and cylinders in the oddest colors. He took a bite of everything, trying to guess which was a fruit and which was a vegetable. A long red pointed tube tasted like an orange crossed with a plum, while a round yellow orb with smooth skin, resembling a tomato, tasted vaguely of carrot and celery. All of it was delicious, except for a purple leaf cluster, like a mini head of lettuce, which tasted faintly of liver.

When he finished, Stewart sat back and looked around the room. Stone walls, thatch roof, vent hole in the center. This can't be happening, he thought. His home, his mom, his friends, even the bullies. They were real. But this? Maybe he was dreaming. Maybe he had gotten hit in the head by an asphalt chunk thrown into the drain by the bullies and would soon wake up, maybe in a hospital. That would certainly be better than being in this place.

With a yawn, Stewart stood up. He wasn't going to figure it out now. He might as well get some sleep. Stewart took the torch down from the wall and shoved it into the bucket. The sand was firm and the lit end did not immediately extinguish. Stewart started to twist the handle to dig the head in, but the flame, licking up the inverted handle, singed his hand. He yanked it away, then drove the torch into the sand by stepping on the end with the sole of his shoe. His hand stung with pain and his skin slowly turned red. Bitopia was most certainly real.

Stewart climbed onto the cot and pulled the coarse blanket over him. He reached out and ran his hand over the cold stone of the wall. He wondered how many boys and girls had spent the same first night in Bitopia on the same cot. Stewart rolled over and shut his eyes. He rolled onto his other side, but he couldn't get comfortable.

He rose from the cot and pushed aside the cloth covering the window. In the circle of night sky framed by the top of the wall floated a moon, pale yellow in color, surrounded by brightly shining stars. Stewart studied the moon, but it certainly didn't look like the same one that orbited Earth. He scanned the stars, wondering if one of them was Earth.

A flash streaked across the sky, a shooting star. Stewart wondered if the citizens of Bitopia had considered flagging down a passing spaceship. But no, that was silly; most of them had probably never heard of a spaceship. Bitopia might not be in the same solar system as Earth, and even if it was, how in the world with their stones and coarse cloth and handmade furniture could they signal a spaceship? As much as he hated to admit it, he was stuck there like all the other children, destined to spend what could be an eternity trapped within the wall, never growing up or older, until the day of the final battle.

CHAPTER 9

Stewart was awoken by the sound of birds. It was not the chirping specifically that brought him out of his slumber. Rather it was the way the chirping sounded, as though the birds were in a canyon. Stewart rose from the cot and went to the window. The sky was blue and cloudless. Every now and then, a bird would fly over the city, its cries echoing off the interior of the wall.

He stared out, across the city. He still couldn't believe he was in this place. He felt like he had gone on an overnight field trip, and today the bus would come pick him up. It just didn't feel real. There had to be a way home, there just had to be.

A knock sounded on the door, and Stewart opened it. A girl stood in the hallway holding a tray of food. She smiled at Stewart and he took it with a murmur of thanks. She bent down and removed the tray from the prior evening. Leaving the door ajar, Stewart set the tray down in the middle of the room and ate. He was halfway through his breakfast when Cora appeared in the doorway, holding a small bundle in her hands, made of the same fabric as her clothes.

"Good morning, Stewart," she said. "May I come in?"

"Sure," he said. "Are you hungry?"

"Oh no, thanks," she said. "I already made a run to the valoire bushes, which grow on a hillside a few thousand paces riverback. They're those long things on your tray, the greenish things. I always eat when I'm gathering, so I don't have to carry my own food back."

"What's 'riverback'?" Stewart asked.

"That's the direction," Cora said. "River to your back, in relation to the city. 'Riverleft' means you head away from the city with the river on your left. 'Riverright' is the opposite direction. 'Riverfront' means you cross the river, going away from the city. It's our system for direction."

"Why not north, south, east, west?" Stewart asked.

"We have no compass," Cora said. "Nor a sun."

Stewart mulled that over while chewing on a valoire. "How do you tell time?" he asked.

"Shadow shifts. A shadow will swing from one side of a tree to the other in the course of a day. We divide that arc into eight parts. So mid-day is four shadow shifts, end-day is eight."

"What happens," Stewart asked, "if it is cloudy, or you wake up after the daylight starts and can't tell the starting point of the shadow?"

"If it's cloudy, then we guess the time based on hunger. If we wake up late, we still know the time because the shadows always follow the same arc." Cora smiled. "I'm so happy you are asking these questions. Not every Newcomer is so eager to learn about Bitopia. Some Newcomers cry for days. But there's so much to learn, and I think you'll love it here.

"And we have a big day planned. Today I'm going to show you around and show you some of the things that we do so you'll understand the different roles. Eventually, you will choose a role, as all citizens have to contribute. Your role will be based on what skills you have and what you want to do. If you are fast and cunning, you can be a Gatherer, like me. If you like making things out of wood, you can be a Crafter. The Masons are generally strong and like working with stones and mortar. The Weavers turn the lylan vines and fluff plants into cloth from which our clothing is made. And there are many other roles.

"But speaking of which," she said as she unfolded the bundle she was holding. She held up pants, a shirt, and a pair of shoes, identical to her own, as well as a small coil of vine. "I've brought you your clothes."

Stewart looked at the clothes, then at his own. "I'm fine in my own clothes, thanks," he said.

"You have to change. Everyone must wear Bitopian clothes. It's the law."

"Why?" Stewart asked.

"For safety," Cora said. "The Bitopian clothes blend in."

"Are we going outside?" Stewart asked, suddenly fearful.

"No, not at all," Cora said. "Don't worry, we're all perfectly safe in here. It's just that, well, it's just the law, that's all. You have to change."

Stewart suddenly remembered the day he went shopping with his mom for the outfit, which they had gotten just after arriving in Harrison City. It was the first department store they had found in their new city, and after shopping, they were both hungry, but the only place nearby with food was an ice cream store. So they had an ice cream lunch. He felt a lump form in his throat at the memory.

"What will you do with my clothes?" he asked.

"They'll stay here, in your room, with you, for now, until you choose a role and get your own living quarters. I know this is hard," she said gently. "But trust me, it's easier this way, easier for everyone."

Stewart finished eating and, with Cora waiting outside, changed into the Bitopian clothes. To his surprise, the fabric was far softer than he had expected. And the shoes, while soft, had thick soles and would protect his feet. After Cora showed him the best knot to use for the vine that held up his pants and shoe tops, they headed out.

Despite the brightness of the sky above, the air carried a slight chill, cooled from the stones of the wall. Outside the wall, Stewart figured, the day must be warm and bright. But the city was cool, dim, and damp.

"Let's start at the well that provides our water," Cora said. "It's in the center of the city."

They walked down a wide straight avenue that led directly from the back of the Curia. In the distance, Stewart could see that the avenue led to a fountain. The cross streets they passed curved, and every now and then they came to a low wall, twenty to thirty feet in height.

"The city is organized in a series of concentric circles, seven in all, delineated by the smaller walls," Cora said, sounding like a tour guide. "So we have ring roads, which go in circles, and spoke streets, which run straight from the center of the city to the wall.

"Although we can't be certain," Cora said as they passed through an archway in one of the stone walls, "we believe that these smaller, inner walls are older than the big city wall and show the growth of the city. As the city population grew, a new wall was built, farther out, and new houses were built behind it."

The buildings did appear to get older as they approached the city center. Whereas the Curia was built of similarly sized stones evenly spaced with mortar, the stones in the buildings became more uneven and haphazardly placed the closer they got to the fountain. Rooflines became wavy, some walls leaned out toward the street, others bowed slightly or were of varying height along the top. The window and door openings, straight and square in the outer Rings, were more crooked in the older buildings.

"Why are all the houses so dark?" Stewart asked.

"Torch use is restricted to official business in the Curia only. Same with fires. If everyone used torches then the city would get too smoky. We didn't always have that problem, but as we built the wall higher, the smoke got trapped inside. The Potters used to make cups and bowls from fired clay, but the ovens generated too much smoke. We tried to rebuild the ovens outside the city wall, but the Venators destroyed them. So now we make dishes and vessels out of wood, and the Potters had to take on other roles."

They reached the fountain, which stood in a central plaza paved by smooth, flat stones. Unlike the decorative fountains in Harrison City, this fountain was clearly built with a purpose. Made completely of stone, a central spout about ten feet high sent water flowing down a stone channel that divided and fed two rectangular basins set about three feet apart.

Behind the fountain, a boy and a girl worked a pump, a wooden beam with connecting rods that they moved up and down like a seesaw. Another girl appeared to be watching the water level in the rectangular basins and now and then would say something to the children working the beam, who would increase or decrease the speed of the pump.

In a line leading to the rectangular stone basins, children stood with wooden crossbars on their shoulders, attached to the ends of which were wooden buckets tied with coarse rope. Each child would walk between the stone basins, crouch down so that the buckets dipped into the water, then slowly stand up, lifting the filled buckets clear of the basins. A steady stream of children with full buckets headed off into the city while ones with empty buckets returned at just as steady a rate.

"That's the Pump Master," Cora said, pointing to the girl watching the basins. "She regulates the speed of the Pumpers so that the water in the basins is kept at the proper level. Everyone with buckets is a Carrier. They deliver water to all the cisterns so that each house has running water."

Stewart marveled at the order with which everyone worked. No pushing, no bumping, no cutting ahead of the line, no one complaining. But then he realized that they all had to; if the city was to have running water, they had to carry it to the houses. There was no time for games, silliness, or arguing.

"If you like walking around the city, a Carrier would be a perfect role," Cora said. "However, you would have to take on another role eventually as the Princeps wants us to build an aqueduct system so that water can flow to all parts of the city instead of being carried. Once the Inventors have the design worked out, the Masons are going to build it. It would be a huge honor to build the aqueduct. Come on, let's go to the stone-working center where the Masons are, and we can stop at the Woodshop on the way to see the Crafters."

They left the fountain on a spoke street, headed toward the wall. They came to the Woodshop, an open shed with just a back wall and a sloping roof. In the back of the shed, a group of Crafters split logs into boards with sharpened stone axes and wedges and then removed the bark with stone hatchets and adzes. The boards were then handed to another group of Crafters, who scraped the rough boards with stones to make them smooth before putting them on a pile. At tables around the rest of the shop floor, Crafters assembled various objects, carving pieces, drilling holes with stone-tipped augers, and connecting the parts with wooden pegs.

In one corner, a Crafter was spinning a board on a foot pedal-driven lathe, rounding the wood into a large disk. After he shaved the wood down, he stopped the lathe, and then attempted to fit a round black ring around the disk.

"What's he doing?" Stewart asked.

"He's making a wheel," Cora said.

"Where did he get the tire?" Stewart asked.

"The Inventors made it. They're tasked with trying to make new things based on the materials we have at hand, such as the charsticks we write with, and improving the things we already have, such as the wheelbarrows. That tire is made out of ulunga tree sap mixed with vine fibers, the same fibers we use for making rope. That wheel is for a wheelbarrow, used by the Masons to transport stones. Until the Inventors developed tires, the Masons had to drag the stones on sleds, which was tiring, not to mention that the sleds wore out pretty quickly on the street cobbles."

Working in the Woodshop certainly looked like fun, Stewart thought. He liked the smell of the fresh wood and the sound of the scraping, hacking, and pounding. But something bothered him about the scene. Something wasn't right. Then he realized it; all the children were working with sharp tools, yet there wasn't an adult in sight. They truly were all on their own.

After the Woodshop, they continued toward the wall. They came to a large open area at the base of the wall, next to a port, that contained piles of stones, a large water basin, an area delineated by a low curb and filled with a thick, creamy paste, and heaps of sand and clay hunks.

The first thing that struck Stewart was the sight of the Masons' muscular arms. Most of the Masons appeared to be his age, but their arms were bulging and powerful. Of course, he realized; the Princeps had been in the city for over a hundred years. Some of the Masons may have been there almost that long. Years and decades spent moving stones would certainly make a person stronger.

Some Masons were sorting stones by size and shape while others loaded crude wooden wheelbarrows. Some were taking measures of sand and hunks of clay, mixing them with water from the basin, and then mashing them together with wooden paddles in the area delineated by the curb.

"What are they doing?" Stewart asked Cora, pointing to the Masons making the paste.

"They're making mortar, which holds the stones together and keeps the stones from cracking under the weight of the stones placed on top. The Gatherers get sand from the river and clay from a hill four hundred paces riverright, and then the Masons mix it together. That's why they work next to a port, so they can send Gatherers out to get more supplies when needed."

"The Gatherers bring the stones too?"

"No," Cora said. "We send out a wagon to get the stones, so we can get a load at a time."

Stewart studied the port, wondering how the wagon fit through.

Cora guessed what Stewart was thinking and laughed. "We use the front gate," she said. "That's how we get wood in as well. But we rarely open the gate, as the large opening is harder to defend than the ports. All other times we keep the gate locked tight."

Stewart nodded. It made sense. "So the Masons can send out the Gatherers?" he asked.

"Yes," Cora said. "Everyone works together. For example, the Inventors work with the Masons to improve the mortar formula. The latest formula only takes seven days to fully dry, and is thick enough so that you can build a full-height wall all at once, a big improvement over the formula described in the *Comlat*, which took twice as long to dry and was pretty thin so it only allowed you to build two or three stones high at a time until the mortar hardened. And the Crafters help build better wheelbarrows for the Masons to move their stones, using the tires made by the Inventors. The Masons help the Pumpers and Carriers by ensuring that the seams of the fountain and water buckets are sealed with clay so they don't leak. The Gatherers, of course, get everyone's food as well as supplies for the Masons, Crafters, and Weavers. The Sorters ensure the food is consumed at the right time and stored properly, and the..."

Cora, looking at Stewart's face, stopped. "This is a lot for your first day, and you must be hungry. Let's take a break and have something to eat. And," she said with a smile, "I want to show you one of my favorite places."

CHAPTER 10

Cora led Stewart to the Food Store, picked up a basket of berries, vegetables, and long, flat, brown chunks that looked like tree bark, grabbed a woven reed mat from a stack in one corner, and led him to the base of one of the wall's towers. They passed through a narrow doorway and started to ascend the dimly lit stairway, the circular windows on the city side marking their progress. The climb was long and tiring, but a current of air flowed up the stairway, keeping them cool.

At the top, they stepped out onto a wide stone walkway bordered on each side by a low stone bulwark. The brightness from the daylight caused Stewart to blink and shield his eyes until they adjusted. But the view from the great height of the wall was stunning.

The landscape was covered with sweeping forests and fields, the river a ribbon of blue winding between them. The colors of the land were vibrant; brilliant greens of the grasses, the rainbow hues of the bushes and trees. The mountains hovered at the edge of the horizon, ringing it all in. Stewart felt as though he were staring out upon a great big bowl of emerald green ice cream sprinkled with colorful candies.

"Isn't it beautiful up here?" Cora asked.

In the sky, almost to the horizon, Stewart spied a dark spot, which grew larger by the second. As it came closer, he saw that it was a bird, like an eagle or a hawk, but larger than he had ever seen.

"What's that?" he asked Cora.

She looked up from where she was spreading out the food on the mat.

"That's Falcon," she said. "Bitopia is filled with all sorts of creatures, most of them enormous. The Gatherers see them now and then when our paths cross."

"I saw a big deer when I arrived yesterday," Stewart said.

"That's Stag. He's always ambling about in the fields on the other side of the Far Wood. I've also met Tortoise, Rabbit, and Fish, who's about six feet long and lives mostly in the Bottomless Lake. Believe it or not, some of these creatures can talk. We don't interact much with them though. When we're outside the wall we always have to keep moving to avoid the Venators."

Stewart followed the river with his eyes. Upstream from the city, the river coursed a relatively straight but meandering line, then hooked sharply to the left, toward the mountains, before disappearing from view. In the downstream direction, the river widened, passing through fields and forests. The river eventually was hidden by trees, but in the far distance Stewart spied a wide bit of blue, which he assumed was the Bottomless Lake.

From down below in the plain surrounding the city came a faint scream. Cora jumped up and stared over the bulwark.

"Oh, no!" she shouted.

Stewart joined her and looked down. At first he didn't know what Cora was looking at, but then movement around a group of bushes near the river caught his eye. A young girl was trying to escape from a Venator. The Venator was trying to grab the girl, who was dodging left, then right, then racing around a bush. The girl could easily dodge the creature, but when she started running straight toward the wall, the Venator, with its long legs, closed in. Just when it seemed that the Venator would grab her, she turned sharply and ran around a bush. The girl was making her way from bush to bush, getting closer to the wall each time but barely avoiding the swinging hands of the Venator. Stewart stood frozen, both horrified and fascinated by the sight of the Venator.

"Come on, Gretchen, you can make it!" Cora shouted.

Cora was rigid, standing on her tip toes, her hands balled into fists, cheering when Gretchen opened a gap with the creature, tensing when the creature closed in and made a grab. Finally, Gretchen cut sharply to the right and the creature lost its footing, falling to the ground. Gretchen then raced straight for the wall, disappearing into a clump of trees at the base.

"Yes!" Cora said, pumping one fist in the air. "That was close!"

Stewart watched the Venator rise to its feet and lope away, disappearing into a nearby forest.

"Lucky for Gretchen, it was a slow one," Cora said. "I thought she was a goner."

"What would have happened if she had gotten caught?" Stewart asked, shuddering at the thought of that huge creature's hands, the sinewy but muscular arms, the snarling face.

"Bad things," Cora said. "Lots of bumps and bruises. Pulled hair. Twisted arm. Maybe a bloody nose. She would have been out of commission for a couple of days at least."

"So they just hurt you and let you go?" Stewart asked, surprised.

"Pretty much," Cora said. "But it's a really frightening experience as you never know what they'll do. That's probably the worst part, not knowing when they'll be finished with you."

"So no one ever gets killed?" Stewart asked.

"Oh no," Cora said. "Sometimes they don't even hurt us that badly. But it's really scary. They're not pretty to look at. And they smell terrible. Of course, they usually only appear one at a time when we're out gathering. If you ran into a gang of them, or a whole invading force when they lay siege to the city, you probably would get killed. But yeah, they pretty much seem to just want to hurt us."

"That's so strange," Stewart said. "I wonder why."

"You know," she said, "I never really gave it much thought. I guess I've been too busy running from them. But it's a weird world, so I guess it has weird creatures."

She left the bulwark, knelt down on the walkway, and began spreading out the food on the mat.

"Maybe they see us as invaders of Bitopia and don't want us around and think by hurting us that we'll leave," Stewart suggested.

"Maybe," Cora said.

"If only we could go home," he said quietly.

Stewart stood for a moment more, then walked to the opposite bulwark and looked down into the city. The daylight only reached halfway down the wall on one side, rendering the entire city in shadow. The thatch roofs were mottled yellow splotches between the greenish and brown stones of the streets and ring walls. He could see the citizens moving about below, carrying out their tasks. He looked back out at the landscape, then back down at the city. Such a shame, he thought, to have all these strange and beautiful lands and creatures outside the wall but be forced by the Venators to stay inside the city. In a way, they were imprisoned in the city, the Venators their jailors.

"Come on," Cora said, gesturing toward the food spread out before her. "Excitement's over; let's eat."

Stewart sat down next to the mat and they both ate. He recognized some of the fruit, and the bark-like food was like a cross between a hard bread and a thick, multigrain cracker. As he munched, Stewart thought about the Venator chasing Gretchen and how Cora said that they only hurt the citizens.

"What exactly happened to the Forebears?" Stewart asked.

Cora finished chewing a fober fruit. "They all died. When the Venators got into the city, they must have chased the Forebears outside. When they lost the safety of the wall, they had to fend for themselves out in the wild while trying to fight off the Venators. So they all must have died of exposure or starvation. I can't imagine trying to survive outside the wall without some form of protection. You would never be able to rest, even for a moment."

"But how do you know that they all died?" Stewart asked.

"We never saw any outside the city. And I've been all the way to the Outer Reaches, at the base of the mountains, a number of times."

"Did you find any houses or makeshift shelters?" Stewart asked.

"No," Cora said.

"Nothing?" Stewart asked, surprised. "What about the other Gatherers, have they seen anything?"

"No, they haven't either. We all share information about anything new we encounter so that no one is ever surprised out there. Knowledge of the landscape, especially new and previously undiscovered features, is critical to everyone's survival."

"How many Forebears were there?" Stewart asked, thinking that perhaps there weren't enough to leave any trace behind.

"We're not sure, but we suspect, based on the number of houses in the city that appeared to have been occupied, at least a few hundred."

"A few hundred?" Stewart asked. "And you found no sign of them?" That didn't seem possible. "What about," Stewart said, wincing, "any bodies, or bones?"

"Not that I know of," Cora said. "I've found small animal bones, but nothing ever human-sized and certainly no skulls. But maybe it was so long before the Princeps came that all the bones washed away or something."

Stewart thought about a TV show he saw on bones found in Africa that were millions of years old. "Washed away to where?" Stewart asked.

"How should I know?" Cora asked.

"I would have expected there to have been bones somewhere," Stewart said.

"Maybe the Venators cleaned them up," Cora said.

Stewart pondered that idea. "Do they really strike you as neat and clean?" he asked.

Cora laughed. "More like messy and smelly!" She grabbed a small red globe, the size of a cherry tomato but with a reddish purple skin like a plum. "Here, try this, we call them squirt poppers."

"Why?" Stewart asked.

"Just put it in your mouth and chew," she said.

Stewart put the fruit in his mouth and bit down. The skin resisted his bite at first, then, with an audible pop, he burst through the skin into a juicy interior. The force of the fruit bursting caused a stream of juice to squirt out his mouth.

Cora fell over with laughter. "Look at your face!" she said. "You weren't expecting that, were you."

Stewart laughed too, the juice dripping down his chin.

When they finished eating, Stewart stood up and looked out over the landscape. He wondered what his mom was doing at that moment. She was probably frantic that he hadn't come home last night. She would have called the police and, knowing her, the fire department as well, and would be driving around the neighborhood looking for him. And everyone at school would know he had gone missing.

Stewart was suddenly struck by a thought—maybe, just maybe, the police investigators would interview the Rage, who might tell them about him going down into the drain. Perhaps they would send a search party down who would find his backpack and know that he was somewhere lost in the pipes. They would search and find this world and then figure out how to bring him home.

Cora joined him at the bulwark and stood next to him for a few moments, studying his face. "I know," she said finally. "When I first got to Bitopia, I used to come up here every day to this exact spot, and think, 'There is no way I can be stuck here, that I can't get home.' I was sure that I would be able to see some sign of home, a light or some object on the horizon. Or perhaps a Zeppelin would get blown off course by a storm and would come drifting over the mountains, and then land and all of us citizens would climb aboard and go home. But the Zeppelin never came."

Stewart realized that his dream of being rescued was hopeless. "I really miss home," he said, choking back a tear.

Cora put her arm around his shoulder. "But this place isn't so bad, you'll see. And look how beautiful it is."

But no one can enjoy it, Stewart thought darkly. If it weren't for the Venators, the world that they were trapped in really wouldn't be too bad at all. It would actually be fascinating, completely amazing. Instead, they were all trapped in the dim and damp city, unable to enjoy the warmth, the color, and the adventure that lay outside the wall. At the moment, he couldn't imagine ever thinking of Bitopia as home.

CHAPTER 11

When they had finished eating, Stewart reluctantly followed Cora down the tower stairs. To be perfectly honest, he had no further interest in seeing more of the city. He just wanted to go back to his cot and lie down. But he knew that sulking was not going to get him home.

They spent the rest of the afternoon walking around the city, visiting the Weavers and the Tool Makers and the Inventors. As far as Stewart could tell, the citizens had all their needs covered, from food to clothing to shelter to supplies to crafted goods to the tools to make everything. They even had an Infirmary staffed by Medics where the citizens could go if they felt sick or got a bad scrape, cut, or rash, and where the unlucky Gatherers recovered from encounters with Venators.

While walking through the city, on their way to see the front gate, Stewart noticed a building that was different from the others. Instead of a thatched roof like all the other buildings, this building had a roof made completely of wide flat stones, layered like shingles. The building had no windows, only a single wooden door. Next to the door stood a Defender.

"What's that building?" Stewart asked.

"That's the Vault," Cora said, "where the *Comlat* was found and where we store it for protection."

"Can we go in and see it?" Stewart asked.

"No one is allowed in there," Cora said. "Only the Princeps can access the book."

"Why?" Stewart asked.

"Without it, we wouldn't have been able to survive. Think about how disastrous it would be if it gets lost, or if someone spills water on it, or if it were to burn. And the Forebears didn't have charsticks, they apparently used charcoal, so much of the important writing could easily be erased from the page. Anyone who breaks that law and touches the book gets the worst possible punishment."

"What's that?" Stewart asked.

"Exile. On your own, out with the Venators. No more help from the other citizens, no more safety of the wall."

"Has anyone ever been banished and exiled?" Stewart asked.

"Are you kidding?" Cora said. "No one would dare take that risk. You wouldn't last a day on the outside. You'd be on the run, chased by the Venators, until you'd drop from exhaustion. Even if you could hide, you'd need to make your own shelter, find food, water....I can't imagine it."

Stewart nodded. That certainly was one law he wouldn't break.

As they stood there, a Mason approached with a wheelbarrow loaded with stones. He pushed it over to a small pile of stones that sat against one wall of the Vault, tilted the wheelbarrow to the side, and dumped the stones onto the pile.

"Does the Vault need to be repaired?" Stewart asked. As far as he could tell, it appeared to be in good condition.

"Those stones are to seal off the Vault in case the Venators attack and a breach of our defenses is imminent," Cora said. "We want to make sure they can't destroy the *Comlat* if they get into the city. Just like there were children here before us, more children may come to the city after we're gone. Like the Forebears, we want to preserve and pass on the knowledge that helped us to survive. Part of the Third Prophecy planning directives."

"Aren't there other copies of the book?" Stewart asked.

"We don't know how to make paper," Cora said. "The Inventors are working on it, but they haven't succeeded yet. So we have to protect the book."

"Makes sense," Stewart said, studying the building. The stones were old and weathered, and the mortar was dark, almost black. Around the door, though, Stewart noticed that some of the stones and mortar were lighter in color.

"Is that where you broke through when you noticed the Vault?" Stewart asked, pointing to the door.

"Yes," Cora said. "You can see how the stones and mortar are different from the ones around it. That's also how you can tell where an original building has been repaired."

Stewart nodded and studied the doorway. The newer mortar was reddish-brown in color, different from the tan mortar he had seen the Masons mixing earlier that day. Must have been the original formula from the *Comlat*, Stewart thought, not the improved formula that Cora had mentioned. The original formula...

"Wait a second," Stewart said. "This morning when we visited the Masons, you said that the original mortar formula in the *Comlat* took two weeks to dry and only allowed a two- to three-stone wall height until dry, while the newest formula that the Inventors concocted only takes a week and allows for a full-height wall to be built at once."

"That's right," Cora said.

"But if the Forebears could only build a wall two to three stones high at a time, how did they manage to build the Vault before the Venators got into the city?"

"I don't understand what you're asking," Cora said.

"If the Venators were on the verge of breaking into the city, and the Forebears decided to build the Vault to protect the *Comlat*, wouldn't it have taken a few months to make the building?"

"The Vault itself was probably already built," Cora said. "They just needed to seal off the opening."

"Even so, if the opening was the size of a normal doorway," Stewart said, "it still would have taken some time to fill it in with stones, right?" Stewart silently counted the number of stones from the bottom of the doorway to the top. "The door is about twelve stones high. Three stones every two weeks and it would have taken at least two months to seal the Vault."

"Well, maybe..." Cora broke off, mulling over Stewart's words.

Stewart continued to study the opening. The more he thought about it, the more it made sense.

"So how could the Forebears have known that they were going to be defeated if it would have taken them so long to seal the vault?" Stewart asked. "I would think that they only would have known they were going to be defeated at the last moment, and then there'd be no time to seal the Vault."

"I don't know," Cora said. "That's just what the Prophecy says."

"Really?" Stewart asked. "Have you read it?"

"Well, no, but that's what the Princeps and Lester say. They've read it."

Stewart studied the doorway, then looked out at the encircling wall. He tried to imagine the city under siege, then a moment when all appears lost and then...a few citizens get out some stones and mortar and start piling stones a few at a time and then sit back to wait for the mortar to dry?

"Cora," Stewart said slowly, a sudden thought dawning on him. "What if the Third Prophecy has been misinterpreted? What if the Venators hadn't defeated the Forebears? What if the Forebears had won?"

"No," she said. "That didn't happen. They were all defeated. It had to be."

"But they wouldn't have had time to seal the Vault," Stewart said. "And you said yourself that no one has ever found a trace of them anywhere. No bones, no shelters, nothing that suggests that they hid out in Bitopia. The Forebears had to have won."

"But then where did they all go?" Cora asked, challenging Stewart's point. "If they won, why didn't they just stay in the city?"

Stewart opened his mouth to answer, then closed it. It was a good question, and he didn't have an answer. If there was no trace of the Forebears in Bitopia, and they weren't in the city, then where could they have gone? The realization struck Stewart like a bucket of building stones. For a moment he couldn't speak. Finally he said, "Maybe they all went home."

Cora stared at the Vault, her eyes wide. Then she shook her head, slowly at first, then more quickly. "No, that didn't happen."

Stewart felt a surge of almost overwhelming hope. "Yes! Yes!" he shouted. "Think about it logically," Stewart said, jumping up and down. "If—"

"No, it couldn't have happened!" she shouted. "It just couldn't!" Tears burst from her eyes and she took off running into the city.

"Cora, wait!" Stewart shouted, his joy turning to confusion. "What's wrong?"

He took off running after her, but Cora, knowing the city better and being a Gatherer with lots of practice evading pursuers, soon disappeared from sight.

Stewart wandered the city, wondering where she had gone. He went back to the Curia, but she wasn't there. He asked other citizens that he encountered if they had seen her or knew where she was, but no one had.

Stewart found out where she lived, a small stone building, and called to her through the curtained windows. There was no reply, and although he knew he was intruding and showing disrespect for her privacy, he pushed a curtain aside just a crack so he could see in. Her house had two rooms, a front room with a table and two chairs and a small sleeping alcove in the back. She wasn't home.

Stewart stepped away from her house and turned slowly in a circle. The light of the day cut at an angle, illuminating the wall on one side of the city, the line of light and shadow rising at an angle until it reached the top of the wall on the opposite side, as though the city were a mug of molasses tilted on its side. The area of the city beneath the wall that was fully shrouded in shadow was the darkest, so Stewart decided to head in that direction. If he were upset over something, that's where he would go.

When he reached the base of the wall, Stewart came to a small, narrow building with a roof that sloped at an angle down to the ground. Stewart pushed aside the curtain that served as the door and discovered a stairway that led down under the ground. He descended, guided by the dim light from the doorway, and at the bottom came to another, heavier curtain.

He pushed the curtain aside and a gentle wave of cool air washed over him. The dim shaft of light from the entry behind him illuminated part of a small room. On shelves lining the far wall, Stewart recognized crates and trays of fruits and vegetables from the Food Store. He realized that he had found the Cold Store that Cora had mentioned when he first arrived at the city.

"Cora?" he whispered.

He opened the curtain wider. He didn't see her. He turned to leave when he heard a sniffle.

"Cora?" he whispered again.

"Leave me alone," came her voice from the darkness.

Stewart crept into the room. His eyes adjusted to the dim light, and he found her sitting in the darkest corner, her arms wrapped around her knees, which were pulled up to her chest. He could see tear trails glistening on both cheeks. She looked at him for a moment and then resumed staring out ahead of her.

"Why are you so upset?" Stewart asked.

"Go away," she said.

"I don't understand," Stewart said.

Cora didn't answer, but continued staring. Stewart waited, but when she didn't answer, he figured it might be best if he gave her some time alone. He got up to go.

"I'm over eighty years old," Cora said quietly.

Stewart slowly sat back down.

Cora took a deep breath. "That means that my parents are dead, my brothers are dead, my friends are dead, my dog Spritz is dead. Everyone I know and love is dead."

Stewart pondered her words. She was right. Everyone she knew would be dead by now.

"So when you mention home," Cora said, "that's what I'm reminded of." She pointed at his clothes. "That's the reason we make Newcomers change immediately. The clothes you wore when you arrived are a reminder of home, and no one wants to see them." She sighed. "Bitopia is my home now, and everyone here is my family."

"But you might have relatives," Stewart said. "And you can always make new friends. Wouldn't it be better to return home, to whatever awaits you, than to stay here, living this life, essentially imprisoned by the Venators?"

Cora shook her head, not looking at him.

She didn't want to believe that there was a way out, Stewart realized, that getting home was even possible. She believed it was better to stay here. They probably all did. After enough time had passed, no one would want to go back. It would happen to him, too. Eventually he would come to accept Bitopia as home. The fate that befell Cora would be his own. And he'd want to stay forever as well. Unless, of course, he figured out how the Forebears managed to escape.

Cora wiped a tear from her cheek, then looked over at him.

"Don't delude yourself into thinking that you can get home," she said, as though reading his mind. "If the Forebears had really defeated the Venators, they would have written it in the *Comlat*."

"But what if they did," Stewart said, "and no one has recognized it?"

"That book has been studied and studied."

"But what if it's been misinterpreted?" Stewart leaned closer. "Cora, there's no such thing as prophecies, you know that. Nobody can or has ever been able to predict the future. You only accept the Third Prophecy story because that's what you've been told over and over again. Whatever the Forebears wrote in the book had to have been written after the fact, after they knew what had happened. And if they were writing in the *Comlat*, and they sealed it in the Vault, then they were still inside the city. Sealing off the Vault would have taken weeks. The Venators had to have been the ones that were defeated. What if the Third Prophecy actually provides instructions on how to get home?"

"Do you really believe all this?" she asked.

"Yes!" Stewart said. "I know I'm right. And I know I can prove it. I just need to look at the *Comlat*, to find out what it says exactly."

After a few moments, Cora sighed and slowly rose to her feet.

"In that case," she said, "we'd better go see the Princeps."

CHAPTER 12

They waited in the Curia outside the Princeps' office while she finished up with some business. Cora sat on a bench, but Stewart couldn't sit still. Pacing back and forth, he felt as though he were going to burst with excitement. The more he thought about the mortar and the Forebears and lack of evidence that they had died out in Bitopia, the more confident he felt that the *Comlat* had been misinterpreted. It was completely logical. He was sure that the secret for getting home was right there on the page. And as a Newcomer, who hadn't had the idea of the Third Prophecy recited to him over and over until he believed it, he would be able to read the text with fresh eyes, unclouded by preconceived ideas.

The curtain to the Princeps' office parted and a Defender ushered them in. The room contained a table that served as a desk, a stool on one side for the Princeps, and four stools on the opposite side of the table. The Princeps was sitting, looking over two smooth wooden panels that lay on her desk, their surfaces marked up by dark black lines, plans of some kind apparently. Across the top of one of the panels was the word, *AQUEDUCT*.

In her fist the Princeps held a wooden tube that had a small hole in one end and a stick protruding from the other on which her thumb rested. Stewart wondered what it was for until she placed the end with the hole on a panel and pushed on the other end with her thumb, squeezing out a line of black paste. It was a charstick.

The Princeps gestured that they should sit on the stools, made a final mark on the panel, then put the charstick down.

"How are you adjusting?" the Princeps asked, leaning forward and giving Stewart a warm and sympathetic smile.

"Just great, just great," he said, barely able to contain his excitement. "Listen, I think I've found a clue to getting home."

The Princeps sat up slightly. "Really."

"I believe," Stewart said, "that there's been a misinterpretation about the Third Prophecy."

The Princeps glanced at Cora, then turned her attention back to Stewart.

Stewart went on to explain the evidence that he had pieced together, that no trace of the Forebears had been found, how there was no way the Forebears could have predicted what would happen, and how the mortar drying time proved that they were still in the city after the battle was over. "All we need to do is have a look at the *Comlat*," Stewart said. "I'm sure the answer is in there!"

"I understand completely," the Princeps said.

"You do?" Stewart said, elated. "Great! So can we look at the book?"

"Stewart, do you remember how I told you that all of our stories about how we wound up here, in Bitopia, were the same?" she asked.

He nodded, not sure how that was relevant.

"What you are going through now is perfectly normal, something we all went through too. We all refused to accept this place at first, we all looked for clues that might lead us home."

"No, that's not it...." Stewart started to say, but the Princeps held up her hand.

"Coming here is very hard to accept," she continued. "You don't want to be here, and you desperately want to get home. So you find what you believe are clues, you become convinced, and then you come up with a plan.

"When I first got here, I saw how the clouds came drifting over the mountains and thought they looked exactly like the clouds from home. So my plan was to build a steam engine to power us over the mountains to get home. And Cora, you wanted to fly in something, if I remember correctly."

"A hot air balloon," Cora admitted.

"Because?" the Princeps asked.

Cora thought for a moment. "The birds. In a grove of fober trees that I visited when I first became a Gatherer, there was a flock of birds that I swore were the same ones that lived in a park in my neighborhood. They looked the same, the songs were the same, or so I wanted to believe. I thought that if we had a balloon, we could just float up and follow the birds back home."

"That's right," the Princeps said. "So you see, Stewart, what you are going through is perfectly normal. Everyone in their first days or weeks or even months here comes up with ideas like these, signs they think point to a way home. When confronted with the sudden and drastic reality shift, your mind will fight it at first."

"Hold on," Stewart protested. "This isn't some farfetched illogical connection between home and here like similar clouds or identical birds. What I'm saying makes perfect sense! There is no evidence that the Forebears lived outside the city or even died. They had to go somewhere. Why can't that somewhere have been home?"

"We have no evidence that they didn't live outside the city or die," the Princeps said. "Any shelters that they would have built, if they could have while being pursued by Venators, would have been temporary at best. And yes, while we haven't found bones or other remains of the Forebears, we haven't been looking for remains either. The absence of evidence does not make something false.

"And if the Forebears had won, they would have stayed inside the city. They would have repelled the Venators again, for the third time, and would have been biding their time until the fourth assault. So it doesn't make sense that the Forebears would have won and not be here. They aren't here, and so they lost.

"Stewart," the Princeps said, her voice softening. "I wish it were true, too, that the Forebears went home. That would be wonderful. That would mean that there is a way back. But we've explored every inch of Bitopia and studied every line of the *Comlat* and have never found a way."

"But the sealing of the Vault!" Stewart said. "How do you explain that?"

"The Forebears used wooden forms, inside and out, to support the stones. We found remnants of the exterior form, weathered and rotted, outside the Vault and the inside form still in place. Forms allow a wall to be built very quickly, within hours. We used to use forms, but no longer need them due to improvements in the mortar."

She paused to let the explanation sink in.

"So you see, Stewart, we've already thought through these things. Everything you've thought of, some Newcomer before you thought as well. It does you no good to trouble yourself over this. You have to learn to accept Bitopia as home."

"But there are no such things as prophecies!" Stewart said. "You cannot predict the future! You have to agree with me on that."

"The passage in the *Comlat* is called a prophecy because it appears that the Forebears did foretell their own demise," the Princeps said. "I'm sorry, I wish it were not so, but it is. In addition, what happened to the Forebears in the first two battles, as documented in the *Comlat*, parallels our own experience here, which leads many citizens to believe that the third battle will be our demise as well.

"But don't worry," she said quickly. "You should know we're making every possible preparation to ensure that it doesn't happen to us. We've built the wall higher, and reinforced the front gate. We've developed better tools to repel the next attack. Luckily, the Venators are not very sophisticated, and we've always been able to defend against their crude ladders and other attempts to scale the wall. My priority is to ensure that the Third Prophecy does not come to pass."

"So what does the Third Prophecy actually say?" Stewart asked.

"The passage describes how the Forebears defended themselves to the end in the final battle but then were driven out of the city and were dispersed throughout Bitopia where, presumably, they died."

"But that doesn't make sense!" Stewart said. "At the time they sealed the *Comlat* in the vault, even if it only took a few hours, they were still inside the city. All they could have known was that the Venators were about to enter. There is no way they could have predicted the rest."

"But what they predicted is really the only plausible outcome if the Venators were about to enter the city," the Princeps said.

"But not certain," Stewart countered. "And you presume that they died. You don't really know that they did. The absence of evidence does not make something true."

The Princeps sighed. "I don't know what else to tell you, Stewart. You are a Newcomer, and I know this is hard. You deserve to have every question answered, and answered truthfully. That is our policy, and that is what I'm doing. There is nothing more that I can do."

"Yes there is," Stewart said. "You can let me look at the *Comlat*."

"No, I cannot do that," the Princeps replied.

"Why not? Just five minutes. Maybe, just maybe, I'll see something that no one else has."

"Five minutes would do you no good," the Princeps said. "The *Comlat* is very hard to understand. It would take days of study before you could even begin to read it."

"Then you can read it for us," Stewart said. "Read exactly what it says, not what you think it means."

"That would not help you either," the Princeps said. "All the passages in the *Comlat* are cryptic, and require interpretation based on knowledge of Bitopian history."

"And that's my point!" Stewart said, louder than he intended. "The passages have been interpreted. What if they've been misinterpreted?"

"Our interpretations of everything else have been accurate. We have no reason to believe we might be in error with what happened to the Forebears.

"I know this is hard to accept," the Princeps continued, "but I can't give in to this request. If I even entertain this notion and give you the impression you might be right, it will only take that much longer for you to accept this place as your new home."

"No!" Stewart said, more strongly than he would have liked. "I'm not going to accept this place. And I know I'm right!"

The Princeps stared at him for a moment, then sighed. "Let's do this," she said. "Once you are settled in and have chosen your role and are, shall we say, more objective about this, we can revisit the question of reading the *Comlat*. We'll set some time aside, and you and I can look at the book. How does that sound?"

"I am being objective," Stewart said, pounding his fist on the table. "I'm approaching this logically. There are no such things as prophecies as no one can predict the future! And there is no trace of the Forebears! I don't care if you haven't been looking; someone would have found something by now...."

He suddenly realized that he was shouting. From the expression on the Princeps' face, he knew he hadn't convinced her. Stewart slumped down on his stool and hung his head.

"So that's it then," Stewart said. "I can look at the *Comlat* but only after I accept this place as home."

"I'm sorry, Stewart," the Princeps said. "Truly I am. But having studied the *Comlat* more than anyone, and given that these types of ideas are normal for all Newcomers, I have to admit that I don't feel as great a sense of urgency to review the book as you do."

"But I'll never accept this place as home," Stewart said quietly. "And so we'll all be trapped here forever."

Stewart got off the stool and, without waiting for Cora, left the room.

CHAPTER 13

Stewart walked briskly through the city in no direction in particular. He was angry. More than angry. It was bad enough that he was a prisoner in the city, but now he felt like he was being held prisoner by the very people who lived in it. He was right about the Forebears, he just knew it. Whatever was in the *Comlat* had to have been misinterpreted. But there was no way to prove it.

And now he knew that the Princeps, along with everyone else who had accepted Bitopia as home, probably didn't want to go back. Everyone would know that their parents were gone, their friends gone, the world that they knew was gone forever. They probably didn't want him to find a way home. Their unwillingness to face the reality of the passage of time would trap him here forever.

The spoke street he was following led to one of the towers at the wall, which loomed high above him. Looking up from the base, the wall and tower appeared to be leaning over him, as though it might topple at any moment. Blasted wall, he thought. No matter what direction he walked, he would always come to the wall. And if he followed it, it would just take him in circles. He wished he could go outside, go someplace where he could wander in any direction he wished, some place that didn't keep him trapped.

"There you are," Cora said, running up to him.

"Yes, still here. I certainly couldn't have gotten far," he said, glaring at the wall. "And thanks for your help back there," he added sarcastically. "I thought you were on my side."

"I'm sorry," Cora said. "What you say does make sense. But I had to do it. Whenever a Newcomer becomes convinced of a way to get home, we're supposed to bring the person to the Princeps. That's just part of the acclimation process.

"And I know you're disappointed, but once you settle in, you'll be able to access the *Comlat* and read it for yourself. It's just a matter of time."

"But how much time?" Stewart asked. "How in the world can I 'settle in' when I know there's a way to get home but I'm not allowed to find out how until I no longer want to go home?"

The thought of being forced to wait what could be months or years, until he was "objective" as the Princeps called it, made his anger boil. Stewart balled his hands into fists. He wanted to run, to scream, to beat his hands on the wall.

"Come, let me show you something."

"What," Stewart said through gritted teeth.

"Just follow me. It'll be very helpful."

She led him into the tower and they started climbing the steps. From all the walking they had done that day, Stewart was already very tired, so the climb was exhausting. When they reached the top, his legs ached and he was out of breath. He stood on the wall just outside the tower, bent over, hands on his knees, breathing heavily, feeling utterly spent.

"So what did you want to show me?" he asked after he had recovered enough to speak.

"Do you feel better now?" Cora asked.

"Is that what you wanted to show me?" Stewart asked.

"Yes," Cora said. "Seeing how angry you were made me remember when I first got here, so long ago. I had almost forgotten. I was very angry. Angry at the world, angry at everyone, and I hated the Princeps. As our leader, she provided all the direction and guidance, made me take a role, had me move into my house and live by myself. I was glad for it later as it was what I needed, but I hated her at first. I was so angry. So I used to come to the tower and run up the steps to look out over Bitopia, and every time I came up here, I always felt a little bit better until finally I was no longer angry. So whenever you are angry, just climb the steps. You'll feel so much better."

Stewart looked out across the fields and forests, then followed the river with his eyes, to where it hooked sharply and disappeared from view. He turned back to Cora.

"I'm not going to wait for the day that I accept this place as home to figure out how to get out of here," he said, "because that day may never come."

"But what else can you do?" Cora asked.

"I'm going to look at the *Comlat*," Stewart said.

Cora's jaw dropped and she took a step back. "Are you out of your mind?" she asked. "What if you get caught?"

"I have to take that chance," Stewart said.

"That's crazy," she said. "And there's no way you can get into the Vault. It's guarded night and day."

"I can do it," he said. He looked away, then back at her. "But I'll need help."

"No," she said. "No way. Forget it. I'm not going in there and risking exile."

"You wouldn't have to go in, I would. But I will need your help with distracting the guard."

"No!" she said, recoiling slightly. "Even if you do get inside," Cora said, "the Princeps said the *Comlat* was hard to understand. How do you know you can even read it?"

"I'll have to take that chance," Stewart said. "Please, Cora, I can't do this alone."

"No!" she said. "There is no need to risk exile when all you have to do is wait."

"Wait until when?" Stewart asked. "Until I no longer want to go home? No, I have to do it now. Come on, what do you say?"

Cora looked away.

"Please, Cora," Stewart said. "Can you at least consider helping me?"

"No," Cora said. "No!"

"Just think about it. You only have to provide a distraction...."

"No!" Cora screamed.

Stewart was taken aback by the force of her reply, then realized that her gaze was locked on something off in the distance. He turned and looked. At first, he couldn't figure out what she was looking at. Then he saw it. In a forest next to the riverleft plain, Venators were creeping slowly among the trees, headed toward the city. Dozens of them. In their hands they carried sticks, and some had sacks thrown over their shoulders. Stewart felt a knot of fear form in his stomach.

"This is it," Cora said almost breathlessly. "The final battle is upon us."

CHAPTER 14

Cora and Stewart raced down the steps of the tower.

"You notify the Princeps," Cora said as they descended. "I've got to warn the Gatherers not to go out. Do you remember how to get back to the Curia?"

"Yes," Stewart said, his reply coming in multiple syllables from the rapid pounding of his feet on the stone steps.

At the bottom of the tower they burst outside. Cora took off running and soon disappeared from view. Stewart ran toward the middle of the city, his confidence in knowing his way around faltering with the importance of his task. He tried scanning above the rooftops as he ran, but the ring walls blocked his view. He came to a spoke street and remembered that one led from the central plaza with the fountain directly to the Curia. He ran into the plaza, then ran in an arc around it, dodging the Water Carriers, until he saw the spoke street that led to the Curia. He sped down it, through a number of arches in the ring walls, until he reached the front door. He ran inside to an intersection of hallways and then stopped, as he had no idea where to go.

"Princeps Evelyn!" Stewart shouted between gasps. "Princeps!"

He heard the sound of rapidly approaching footsteps. Moments later, the Princeps, followed by Lester and two Defenders, came hurrying around a corner.

"Princeps," Stewart said. "The Venators! They're massing outside the wall."

"How many?" she asked quickly.

"I don't know, dozens," Stewart said. "We saw them moving through the woods."

"Were they carrying anything?" Lester asked.

"Sticks, I think," Stewart said. "Bags and sacks, too."

The Princeps and Lester exchanged glances.

"Where's Cora?" the Princeps asked.

"She went to warn the Gatherers," Stewart replied.

"Smart girl," the Princeps said. She turned to Lester. "Send two Defenders to guard each port. Then meet us on top of the wall. And bring the horn." The Princeps turned to Stewart. "Show me."

Stewart led the Princeps and the two Defenders to the top of the wall and pointed out the forest where he and Cora had seen the Venators. They all stared, but there was no movement among the trees. Where did they all go? Stewart wondered. Had he and Cora just imagined seeing the Venators? For a long time no one said a word. Then one of the Defenders raised his arm.

"There," he said. "Right at the forest edge, closest to the river."

A Venator had stepped out from behind a tree. As they watched, it moved to the next one over. Farther down the forest edge, another appeared and then resumed hiding.

"They're in there all right," the Princeps said.

Lester emerged from a tower farther down the top of the wall and ran toward them. He carried a long white crescent-shaped tube that narrowed along its length. The point on the end was gone, leaving a small hole. It looked like a horn from a Texas steer. When he reached them, the Princeps pointed at the woods.

"They're in there," she said to Lester.

"How many have you seen?" Lester asked.

"Only a couple, but they're following the same pattern as the last two battles, the advance force massing in the trees."

"Any sign of the main force?" Lester asked.

They all stared out into the distance. Stewart didn't know what they were looking for, but he scanned anyway.

"There," Lester said, pointing.

Far beyond the forest, almost out of sight, was what at first appeared to be a dark line. But it was moving, like a snake slithering slowly through grass. As it got closer, Stewart was able to see that it was a column of Venators, hundreds of them, slowly marching toward the city, some pulling wagons, others with bags and sacks in their arms.

"What's that, near the head of the group?" one of the Defenders asked.

At the front of the column came two lines of Venators carrying between them a long straight trunk of a tree. Wooden crossbars had been attached to each side of the trunk at even intervals. The Venators carried the trunk by the crossbars. The end of the trunk had been hollowed out.

"That must be a new type of ladder," Lester said.

"You think so?" one of the Defenders asked. "There is no way they can scale the wall with that. It wouldn't even reach a quarter of the way up."

"I'm guessing they have a few of them and they plan on stacking them," Lester said. "The trunk on top fits into the hollowed-out end of the one beneath, to hold it steady." He broke into a wide smile. "They'll need three or four ladder sections just to reach the top of the wall, and we can easily defend against a single ladder. It would take dozens – and at least forty or fifty trees – to successfully scale the wall. Ha! They'll never get in! We will beat the Third Prophecy yet!"

"But I don't see any more ladder sections," the Princeps said.

For a few minutes, everyone studied the Venator force.

"I'll bet they plan on making the ladder sections here," Lester said. "That would certainly save the work of carrying them."

"I hope you're right," the Princeps said.

Cora appeared, breathless from running up the tower steps.

"There you are," the Princeps said. "You warned the Gatherers?"

"Yes," Cora said. "But there are still two outside, Benjamin and Marjorie."

"Lester," the Princeps said. "Inform the Defenders that they are to secure all ports and begin the battle preparations as soon as those two Gatherers are back inside. Now if you will, sound the horn."

Lester brought the horn up to his lips. He took a deep breath and blew. A low rumbling tone, deep and resonant, filled the air. Stewart felt the sound as strongly as he heard it. The sound echoed off the interior of the city wall, doubling upon itself, making the very stones of the wall vibrate. The sound grew louder and louder until Stewart felt that he was enveloped by it, as though the sound was water and he was submerged. When Lester stopped blowing, the sound echoed out across the landscape before dying out. Even after it had stopped, Stewart felt his body tingling from the vibrations. The air felt charged with electricity.

The battle had begun.

CHAPTER 15

As night fell, the city, which until the horn sounded had been characterized by the slow, steady movement of the citizens carrying out their tasks, came alive with frenetic activity. Defenders carrying long poles with y-shaped ends, which Cora explained were used to push ladders back from the wall, hurried through the darkened streets to the towers. Masons jogged wheelbarrows heaped with stones, which the citizens could hurl down on the Venators, to the base of the tower stairs. Water Carriers, their buckets full and sloshing, raced to fill cisterns before the full Venator assault began, as every citizen would be needed to help defend the city.

Cora and Stewart had gone to the Food Store to help with the sorting of food into ration baskets. Since Stewart wasn't familiar with the different kinds of food, he was tasked with delivering the baskets up to the top of the wall for the Defenders, who would remain there day and night, standing ready to repel the assault.

While Stewart walked to and from the wall with an armload of baskets, he couldn't stop thinking about the Vault. He had to get inside to read the *Comlat*. The answer just had to be in there. But without help, getting in would not be easy. He kept thinking the word "impossible," but every time he did, he drove the word from his mind. If he didn't succeed, he might never get home. He would be forced to live within the confines of the wall forever. And since there was no such thing as prophecies, the only break in the routine would be the periodic battles with the Venators.

Returning from the wall to get a new bundle of baskets, he decided to take a short detour on the ring road that would bring him past the Vault, just to see if the door was still guarded. If not, that might give him some options. He came to the house that stood between the road and the Vault and slowly peered around the corner. A Defender was standing at the door.

Stewart pulled back out of sight and sank to the ground, leaning back against the cool stone wall of the house. How in the world, he wondered, was he going to get in? He could distract the guard and sneak in, but then he realized that the guard would return to his post and he wouldn't be able to get out. The Princeps was allowed inside, but he doubted he could impersonate her.

Maybe Cora was right. It was craziness to think about breaking into the Vault. And what if he couldn't read the *Comlat*? He would be thrown out of the city, and then, if by some miracle he managed to survive, he would have no chance of ever getting home.

Stewart decided it would be best to wait until the battle was over. They were certainly safe inside the city. And when the Venators finally gave up and retreated, or were repelled by whatever the Princeps and Defenders had planned, everyone would then see that the Third Prophecy didn't come true, indisputable evidence that the *Comlat* had been misinterpreted. Certainly the Princeps would let him read the book then.

Wearily, Stewart rose to his feet. He would put the Vault and the *Comlat* out of his mind and focus on helping defeat the Venators. That would be the fastest way to getting a look at the *Comlat* and home. As he started off in the direction of the Food Store, however, he heard a loud crash that stopped him short, a thunderous booming sound that echoed off the city wall.

The crash came again. After a few moments, again. Other citizens nearby had stopped as well, listening.

Crash!

Crash!

Then the other citizens started running in the direction of the sound. Stewart followed. What could possibly be making that noise?

Crash!

Citizens were streaming from the ring roads onto a spoke street that led to the front gate. Stewart ran with the crowd, straining to see over everyone's head.

Crash!

The street ended at a large plaza across from which stood the two tall wooden doors of the gate. The doors were made from massive planks of wood and were held in place by carved wooden hinges with pins the thickness of tree trunks. Two large crossbeams, each made from a squared-off tree trunk, were positioned horizontally across the doors. They were held up by wooden support posts, and their ends were secured in large stone brackets protruding from each side of the gate. Next to the gate stood a small pyramid of crossbeams.

Crash!

The sound was coming from the other side of the doors.

Crash!

With each crash, the doors shook. Something was pounding on the doors.

Crash!

"Stewart! Stewart!"

Stewart turned and found Cora pushing through the crowd toward him. Her eyes were wide with fear.

"What do you think—"

Crash!

"—think they're doing out there?" she asked when she reached him.

Crash!

"Sounds like they're try—"

Crash!

"—trying to break in," Stewart said. "You mean they've nev—"

Crash!

"—never done this before?"

Crash!

"Not like this," Cora said.

"Come on, let's take a look," Stewart said.

They pushed their way though the crowd to one of the towers that flanked the gate and got into a line of Defenders moving inside. They made their way slowly up the steps, the crashing against the gate muffled by the tower stones. At the top, a large crowd had already gathered on the wall directly over the gate, looking down.

Stewart and Cora had to move farther down the wall before they could get right up against the bulwark and peer over the edge.

A ring of bonfires set in the field illuminated the area in front of the gate, where at least a hundred Venators had gathered. About a dozen of them stood near the base of the wall, each one using a large wooden shield to deflect the stones the Defenders were hurling down on them. Two rows of ten Venators, protected by the ones with the shields, held between them the long tree trunk with the handles. The hollowed-out end had been fitted with a large, pointed stone. As they watched, the Venators holding the trunk backed up and then ran forward, the point of the rock aimed right at the doors.

Crash!

The stones of the wall shook with the impact. When the Venators pulled the tree trunk back, a few splinters of wood from the gate doors came with it, falling onto a small pile that had formed on the ground. It wasn't a ladder after all, Stewart realized, but a battering ram. The Venators backed up and rammed again.

Crash!

On both sides of the ram path, Venators were driving a line of pointed poles into the ground and lashing a thick branch from one to the next, creating frames for walls. Stewart didn't understand what they were doing until the Venators started attaching poles across the top, from one wall frame to the other, and lashing thick branches between them. The Venators were building a tunnel-like structure to protect the rammers from falling stones and other hurled objects. And with the river nearby, the citizens wouldn't be able to burn the tunnel down; the Venators would simply extinguish dropped torches or burning logs as soon as they landed.

Crash!

More wood splinters came off. It dawned on Stewart that even if they only broke off a few splinters with each charge, they would eventually break through the gate. And if they did, the citizens would be forced to flee. The Third Prophecy would come to pass.

"Citizens, citizens!" came a loud voice from down below in the city.

Stewart and Cora went over to the city side of the wall and looked down. The Princeps was standing on one side of the plaza, her hands cupped to her mouth.

"Please clear the plaza and resume your tasks," the Princeps shouted. "We—"

Crash!

"—We need to reinforce the gate. Clear—"

Crash!

"—Clear the plaza!"

Slowly the citizens in the plaza departed; the few who remained were directed back to the edges by Defenders. When the plaza was clear, two Defenders carrying heavy wooden mallets came forward and, in unison, knocked away the wooden posts supporting the lower crossbeam. The crossbeam slid down against the door and hit the ground with a thud. The Defenders knocked away the posts supporting the second crossbeam and it fell and stacked onto the first. With the ends held secure in the vertical stone brackets, they had started to create a solid wall of crossbeams across the doors.

Defenders at the top of the wall lowered ropes, and Defenders waiting below tied the ends to one of the crossbeams lying on the pile next to the gate. The Defenders on the wall raised up the crossbeam, positioned the ends in the stone brackets, then slowly lowered it down, stacking it onto the second crossbeam. The ropes were untied and refastened to another crossbeam on the pile. Within minutes, the doors were completely hidden behind a solid wall of crossbeams.

Stewart went back to the exterior side of the wall and stared down at the Venators. Although the crossbeams being used to barricade the gate were thick, they were made of wood. Given enough time, the Venators would be able to drive their ram through a wall of wood a mile thick.

Stewart scanned the top of the wall. It was lined with Defenders, each with the y-shaped pole to repel ladders. But down in the plaza, there was nothing happening. And there were no more timbers lying around to use when the ones in place were broken by the battering ram. Unless there was some defense that was yet to be unveiled, the Venators were going to get into the city.

"Cora," Stewart shouted over the din. "The gate is not going to hold them. They're going to get through, eventually."

She watched as the ram battered the doors of the gate again.

"We need to look at the *Comlat*," he shouted.

"Can't you forget about home for just a moment?" she shouted back. "We're in the middle of a battle! Everyone is going to be needed to help defend the city. You included. And you don't even know if the Forebears went home!"

"You're right," Stewart said, "I admit it, I don't know if the Forebears went home. But I do know that the Forebears did not predict their own annihilation, and did not die, which means they had to have won their third battle. And the fact that the Forebears won, but everyone thinks they lost, proves that the *Comlat* was misinterpreted. So if what you call the Third Prophecy describes the final battle and offers any hints on how to defeat the Venators, we'd better have a look at that book."

Cora looked at him, then down at the gate. The pile of splinters was growing.

"You don't know what the Princeps and Lester have planned," Cora said. "They may have some defense against this."

"Cora," Stewart said, "look at the top of the wall. It's lined with Defenders, ready to repel ladders. And look at the plaza. Nearly empty. Obviously, nobody considered a battering ram. "

After a moment, she looked up at him. "Then let's go talk to the Princeps."

"No," Stewart said. "We already did that. If she wouldn't let me look at the *Comlat* when I first asked, she certainly isn't going to when there's a battle going on.

And she might double the number of Defenders guarding the Vault.

"Cora, you know I'm right. For just one moment, forget about not wanting to go home. Forget about all the time that has passed. Think of the facts, that prophecies don't exist, that besides the book they left behind, there is no evidence of the Forebears in Bitopia.

"Cora, the Venators are going to get into the city. If I'm right, this is our chance to figure out how to stop them. If I'm wrong, exile won't matter since the Venators will drive us out anyway. So what do you have to lose?"

For a long minute, she didn't say a word. "How do you plan on getting into the Vault?" she finally asked.

"I don't know yet, but I'll figure out something. Will you help me? Please?"

She looked back down at the Venators, then nodded slowly. "Okay, I'll help. But if you're wrong about the *Comlat*, and somehow the Venators are defeated or retreat, we're both as good as dead."

CHAPTER 16

Stewart and Cora followed the top of the wall to another tower so they could avoid the commotion in the plaza at the gate. They made their way slowly, as the walkway was packed with citizens, some carrying ladder pushers, others food baskets, a few with sticks and stones. Now and then a citizen approached with a torch, the light reflecting off grim faces. The night was cloudless, and two moons, the yellow one Stewart had seen the night before and a slightly bigger pink one, hung in the sky surrounded by countless stars. The glow of the moons glistened on the smooth stones of the walkway, illuminating the way forward with a pastel light.

They couldn't go down the first tower they came to, as it had been designated up-only. So they had to continue around the top of the wall to the next one. The air in the tower was warm from the heat and breath of all the citizens going down. At the bottom, they took a spoke street through the rings until they reached the one containing the Vault. They followed a ring road until they were only a few buildings away. They crept forward until they came to the house in front of the Vault and peeked around the corner. A Defender stood at attention next to the door.

"Now what?" Cora asked when they pulled back out of sight.

"Let me think," Stewart said.

If only they had something to work with. Stewart looked up and down the road. It was empty except for an abandoned wheelbarrow, most likely from one of the citizens who, like Stewart, had gone to investigate the crashing sound at the gate. How could a wheelbarrow help them carry out a plan? Stewart wondered. Wheelbarrow. Carry.

"I've got it," Stewart said.

"Tell me," Cora said, her excitement rising.

Stewart whispered his plan to Cora, explaining who would do what. "So what do you think?" he asked when he had finished.

"That's crazy," Cora said. "But it just might work. Wait! What about light?"

Stewart hadn't thought of that.

"I know," Cora said. "Wait here."

She ran off and disappeared between two houses. Stewart waited, growing more and more restless with each passing second. A minute later, she reappeared carrying what looked like a short club and a rock.

"Found a torch and flint," she said. "Most houses have a spare set in case of an emergency." She handed them over. "You light the torch by striking the flint against a rock, next to the torch head."

"You mean you just hit this rock on another rock, that's it?" Stewart asked, studying the piece of flint and trying to imagine how the torch head would light.

"Yes, at an angle," Cora said. "Just be careful not to scrape your knuckles. Good luck."

Cora trotted off toward the wheelbarrow. Stewart watched her for a moment, then he headed off in the opposite direction. He walked until he was three or four houses away from the Vault, then turned and crept between two of them to circle around behind the Vault. The crashing against the gate had stopped, the noise replaced by a low hum of activity. Stewart glanced up at the wall. The top edge formed a dark line against the background of the moonslit and starlit sky. From the movement of all the citizens atop the wall, the line looked alive, like a wreath of writhing snakes encircling the city, the occasional pinpricks of torchlight their glowing orange eyes.

When Stewart felt he was far enough away from the Vault, he spied a large flat stone in the wall of a house, held the torch head next to it, then struck the flint above it.

"Ow!" he cried, dropping the flint. He held his throbbing fingers in his hand for a moment. He had scraped the skin on three of his knuckles, which were bleeding slightly. He held them against his pants for a moment to stop the blood, then retrieved the flint.

Holding the flint at a sharper angle, he tried again. Nothing happened. He struck harder. A spark flew from where he struck the stone. He struck again, this time at a sharp glancing angle so the flint would scrape the stone. A shower of sparks. Three more strikes and the torch started to smoke, then a small yellow flame appeared and spread over the torch head.

Stewart left the flint at the base of the wall and headed toward the Vault, approaching it from the back. He kept the torch low so he wouldn't be seen and away from his body so he wouldn't get burned. He felt his already rapid heartbeat quicken further as he drew closer. He tried to quiet his breathing, but his breaths came quickly from his excitement. Fearful of stepping on anything that might make a sound or moving too fast and causing the torch to flicker, he crept as carefully as he could until he reached the back wall of the Vault, the side opposite the door and the Defender standing guard. He took a moment to catch his breath and calm down as best he could, then peered around the corner.

Cora was peeking around the house between the Vault and the road. Stewart waved his hand to give the signal that he was in position. A moment later, Cora stepped out, pushing the wheelbarrow quickly and heading straight for the stones piled next to the Vault. Stewart ducked back out of sight.

"I need a hand!" Stewart heard Cora say to the Defender. "A piece of one of the crossbeam brackets crumbled, and I need to bring these stones to the gate for the repair. Can you please help?"

Stewart quickly stepped around to the side opposite the stone pile, crept along the wall until he reached the corner with the front wall, and carefully peered around it. The Defender was facing Cora, his back to Stewart.

"I have to maintain my post," the Defender said.

"Please, we have to move quickly," Cora said. "The Venators are trying to break through the gate."

"But these stones are reserved for sealing the Vault," the Defender said. "I'm not sure you should take—"

"But these are the Princeps' orders," Cora said with urgency.

Stewart held his breath. The Defender wasn't moving. Cora stood there waiting.

"Look," Cora said, somewhat meekly. "I'm just a Gatherer. I'm not used to moving stones. Someone big and strong like you could really be a big help."

Stewart saw the Defender straighten up and square his shoulders.

"Well," the Defender said, "I guess it wouldn't hurt to lend a hand. Just one load, though."

Cora pushed the wheelbarrow toward the stone pile on the side of the building, out of sight, and the Defender followed. Very slowly, Stewart made his way around to the front of the Vault. He grasped the wooden doorknob and pulled. It wouldn't give at first. Finally, it gave with a creak. Stewart froze, expecting the Defender to come storming around the corner. But at just about the same moment, a stone clunked onto the wheelbarrow. The Defender must not have heard.

"One, two, three!" Stewart heard Cora say. *Clunk.* "One, two, three!" *Clunk.*

Stewart smiled. Clever—she must have heard the sound and was letting him know when there would be sound to cover any noise that he would make. He waited until the next three count, then pulled on the door. The door creaked at the same moment the stone *clunked*. The door opened partway. He waited for the next three count before pulling again. The door opened wide enough. He slipped inside the Vault. On the next *clunk*, he pulled the door closed.

CHAPTER 17

As soon as the door closed, the sounds of the city vanished, replaced by the rasp of Stewart's breathing and the faint pulsing hiss of the torch's flames. The Vault was a simple rectangular room that had an arched ceiling of stone. Stewart had been expecting timbers supporting the slate-shingled roof, like all the other buildings he had seen, but now better understood why the building was called the Vault. With an arched ceiling of stone, the building was essentially impenetrable. The slate on top of the building was just a covering to keep the water off.

In the center of the room stood a stone pillar, on which rested a square stone container. The container appeared to be carved from a single block of granite and had a seam about an inch from the top, the lid. Of course, Stewart thought; if the citizens were so concerned about damage to the book, especially fire, they would put it in the most secure vessel they could devise.

Stewart looked at the torch flame, which cast a flickering yellow light around the room, and decided that he'd better keep it as far from the book as he could. He went to the other side of the room and scanned the walls, looking for an uneven mortar seam or a rock protrusion. He found a large stone that jutted out just where the wall started to curve into the ceiling, forming a crevice. He managed to jam the handle of the torch straight into the crevice. The flame licked the ceiling stones, but since they weren't flammable, they wouldn't burn.

Stewart circled back around the pillar, facing the back wall, so his head and body would not cast a shadow on the box. Very carefully, he lifted the stone lid, which was heavier than he had expected. He set it on the floor and looked inside the box.

At the bottom lay a cloth-wrapped bundle. Very gently, Stewart lifted it out and into the light. He pulled back the layers of cloth. Nestled inside was an old book about eight inches by six inches. The cover was made of a thick cardboard, brown with age. In the center of the cover, in cursive black ink, was written:

Commentarius Latinus
Hugo N. Schumacher, 1869

Comlat for short, Stewart realized. But who was this Hugo? And was the book really from 1869? Stewart had coins that old, so there was no reason why the book couldn't be that old either.

Stewart took a deep breath. This is it, he thought. Somewhere within was the answer to defeating the Venators and, he hoped, getting home. Slowly he opened the cover. The first page contained five lines written in the same cursive script:

Difficile est tenere quae acceperis nisi exerceas.

Repetitio est mater studiorum.

Ipsa scientia potestas est.

Experientia docet.

Carpe diem.

Stewart stared at the page. He recognized the letters, but he had no idea what the words meant. *Acceperis? Studiorum? Est?* All of a sudden, he felt an overwhelming rush of fear. The whole plan assumed that he would be able to read the *Comlat*. The Princeps said it was hard to understand, but she never said anything about it being written in a foreign language. He didn't have that much time either. One torch-worth of time, to be exact; as soon as the torch burned out, he wouldn't be able to see. Sometime after that, since she knew how long a torch would last, Cora would create another distraction by returning and unloading the rocks from the wheelbarrow, saying they hadn't been needed so no one would be the wiser. At that point, he'd have to leave. But what if he didn't get the information by that time? And if they failed...

Calm down, Stewart told himself. Figure it out. He took a deep breath and turned the page. On both pages were columns of word pairs, written in the same black ink. The word on the left of each pair was unintelligible, in the same strange language as the writing on the first page, but the word on the right, he saw, after becoming familiar with the way the curlicues formed the letters, was in English:

anno - in the year

ante - before

bi - two

corpus - body

dies - day

est - he/she/it is

et - and

ipsa - herself

ita - thus/so

sine - without

The lists continued on the next few pages, the words becoming longer the farther he went into the book. Stewart flipped through the pages, scanning the lists, looking for something familiar.

habitare - to reside

trigemini - triplets

testamentum - testament

Latinus - Latin

Latinus! That was in the title of the book. It meant "Latin!" The strange language was Latin! And the words on the pages, he realized, were definitions of Latin words. He searched for "Commentarius." He found it:

commentarius - notebook

The answer left him puzzled. The *Comlat* was a Latin notebook? Stewart couldn't understand it. He was expecting a text all about the history of the city and Bitopia, a journal of the Forebears. An old schoolbook? Then Stewart remembered his clothes, folded in a pile in his room in the Curia. The book must have come through the portal with—Stewart flipped back to the front cover—with Hugo N. Schumacher, in 1869. Hugo must have been holding this book, trying to escape his bullies, when he wound up in Bitopia.

That word—*Bitopia*. Stewart flipped back to the first page of words. *Bi* meant "two." Stewart had heard of *utopia*, which meant "perfect world." *Bitopia* must mean "two worlds." The one of the city, and the one outside the city. All the citizens were trapped in one—dark, dreary, confining—and not able to experience the other—beautiful, colorful, and free. Bitopia.

Stewart plunged on, encouraged and excited that he had figured out the nature of the book. He turned the pages slowly, being careful as they, like the cover, had browned with age and felt brittle. He found the word *venator*, Latin for "hunter." So that's where they got the name, he realized. He saw *princeps*, which meant "the first, chief," as well as *curia*, which meant "court, meeting place." He flipped past the word definitions and came to short Latin sentences. He ignored them, looking for something related to Bitopia.

Halfway into the book, the writing suddenly changed. Instead of fine handwriting in ink, the words were written in thick block letters, like a child writing in crayon, still black in color but faint. Each character looked like it had been scratched onto the page. Stewart gently touched the very end of one of the letters. A little of the black came off on his finger, and the spot where he touched the letter on the page was a little fainter. Stewart rubbed his fingers together, feeling the powdery substance, then leaned closer to the page and sniffed. It smelled like burned wood. Did they write with the ends of burned sticks, or charcoal? It was just a guess, but that would explain why the writing was so fragile and didn't stick to the page. And no wonder the book was so protected; one dunk in a pail of water and the writing would be washed away, the information forever lost.

Stewart studied the letters, which were much easier to read than the cursive ink script. He saw a word he recognized at the end of an entry:

RIVERBACK PAST HILL TALL RED TREES GOOD FRUIT – FOBER

Directions on where to find the fober trees, Stewart realized. And the short, clipped phrases—with crude writing implements and limited room in the book to write, the Forebears couldn't waste space with full sentences.

ITCHING – PINK LEAF MASH WATER MUD PASTE

Next to those words was a triangular shape with rounded corners. A sketch of the leaf that was used to help with itching? Mash and mix with water and mud to form a paste. The Infirmary would likely have that on hand.

MORTAR – RED CLAY RIVER UP BLACK SAND RIVER DOWN BEND RIVER PEBBLES

The old mortar recipe. The more he understood, the more his excitement grew. Stewart scanned the pages, noting entries on weaving cloth and woodworking. It dawned on him that the Forebears, some of whom must have been from the nineteenth century, had known how to do all these things. Life had been different in the days before cars and computers. The Forebears probably knew farming, canning, sewing, and how to make things. Stewart was struck by the thought of how unprepared he would have been if he had been the first to arrive, knowing nothing about how to fend for himself in the wild. Everything he had ever needed he had gotten from stores.

The writing became more precise the further he went into the book, as though the Forebears had refined their writing tools. The wide lines suggested that the

Forebears didn't have anything as advanced as charsticks, but they did manage to put more words on the page. And a good thing, too, as Stewart was nearing the end of the book.

About two dozen pages from the end, Stewart came to lines of text that almost made him jump:

BATTLE LADDERS REPELLED LONG SEIGE HUNGRY FRANKS DEFEATED BUILD WALL HIGHER

So this was the entry on the First Battle with the Venators. Hungry Franks? Were they talking about hot dogs? No, the Franks were defeated, so the Forebears must have called the Venators "Franks." But why Franks? Perhaps they knew a bully named Frank? A big, lumbering monster of a bully? Monster! Frankenstein's Monster! The big, lurching, lumbering Venators were like skinny versions of Frankenstein's monster. But was the book *Frankenstein* so old that the Forebears knew the story? Stewart had no idea, but no matter. What did seem certain was that the Franks/Venators had tried to scale the wall with ladders and the Forebears decided to raise the height of it.

Stewart pressed on. He skipped over entries on making buckets and weaving cloth. He was nearing the end, so he was sure that the answer was close. He found what he was looking for:

2ND BATTLE FRANKS LADDERS FOOD WATER INSIDE WALL TO CLOUDS

Stewart read the lines over a few times, wondering what it meant. Then he figured it out. The Venators again tried to use ladders in the second battle. This time, the Forebears didn't go hungry as they had learned to store food and water in the city. And after the battle, they must have built the wall as high as they could so that they would never have to worry about the Venators scaling the wall with ladders again.

The next few pages were loaded with drawings—building designs, woodworking tools, a simple cart—and construction notes. Stewart studied the images and accompanying text, fascinated by the Forebears' ingenuity. In fact, Stewart had become so immersed in the information that he didn't realize he had come to the last page until he held the final brittle brown sheet between his fingers.

Stewart took a deep breath. He had no idea how to defeat the Venators or how to get home and only had one page left. If the information wasn't on this page, they were all doomed.

The torch was beginning to sputter, the light starting to dim. Time was running out. Stewart turned the page, revealing one final block of text:

TWICE ATTACKED TWICE REPELLED UNTIL THIRD ASSAULT INSIDE THE WALL THEY CAME STAND FAST AND TALL THEN SCATTER WITH THE WIND

Underneath the words, from where they ended to the bottom of the page, was a long wavy diagonal line:

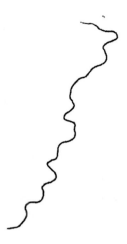

Stewart stared at the text above the wavy line. It was the last entry in the *Comlat*. And it seemed to say exactly what the Princeps described as the Third Prophecy. The third battle, the Venators breached the wall, the Forebears were driven out and scattered across the land.

Stewart, feeling panic rising, started to shake. The light of the torch was sputtering, the flame dying. It was the Third Prophecy.

No! He shouted the word in his mind so loudly that for a moment he wasn't sure if he had actually yelled it. For a horrifying moment, he braced himself for the door to fly open and the Defender to rush in and grab him, but nothing broke the sound of his own breathing and the flickering flame of the torch.

"No," he said, this time in a whisper. Prophecies were not real. The words had to have been written after the Venators had been defeated. There was no way the Forebears could have predicted their own defeat and the aftermath, the scattering across Bitopia. That was ridiculous. They even wrote, "they came." Past tense. It had to have been written later.

Stewart read the words again, slowly and carefully. Twice attacked and repelled—that was the first and second battles. That seemed pretty clear. On the third assault, the Venators entered the city. That seemed pretty straightforward as well. The last lines, then, had to be the key:

STAND FAST AND TALL THEN SCATTER WITH THE WIND

What did that *mean*? Stewart rubbed his temple. His head hurt and his back and legs ached from standing for so long. *Stand fast and tall.* Did the Forebears just stand there when the Venators came in? Is that what they were supposed to do? That made no sense. The Venators would come in and everyone would try to hide or flee. They would be driven out of the city. Scattered with the wind. The passage said just what the Princeps had said it did. But prophecies aren't real! Stewart wanted to scream. There had to be more!

Stewart stared at the line underneath the words. A slight hook at the top, a dot that could have been intentional or accidental next to it, then a long wavy diagonal across the page. A line with a hook and a dot. He had seen something like this before, at the end of journals. A slash across the page to signify that nothing more could be written, usually with a word or phrase such as "*finis*," or "finished," or "the end." It was, in fact, the end.

Without warning, the torch went out.

CHAPTER 18

Stewart sat on the floor in the darkness, his back against the pillar, waiting for the sound of rock clumping from the wheelbarrow onto the stone pile, the signal to sneak out of the Vault. When the torch had gone out, the room had been plunged into darkness, but he could still see a faint crack of light from outside—more like a gray line contrasting with the blackness in the Vault—at the top and bottom of the door.

He didn't know if he should laugh or cry. He had risked everything, for both himself and for Cora, and he had failed. How in the world did he think, that in an hour or so of time, he would be able to see something that others who had studied the book for decades had missed? Maybe the Princeps was right; maybe his mind was grasping onto imagined clues and far-fetched notions as a defense against accepting reality. Maybe he was in denial.

Whatever the case, he had failed to figure out the way to defeat the Venators and the way home. And if they did manage to prevent the Venators from entering the city, he would likely be spending a long time—years, decades, maybe even centuries—in the city, trying to figure exactly how the Forebears managed to escape Bitopia. And there was a good chance that he never would.

But that riddle would have to be solved another day. Right now, he had to get out unnoticed or he and Cora would be in worse trouble than he had ever been in his entire life. He sat listening. Then he remembered the torch. He had to get it out of the ceiling and take it with them or someone would see it the next time the Vault was opened. And the *Comlat* itself; he would have to put it back the same way he had found it.

Stewart stood up slowly in the darkness, feeling the pillar, then the box, then the cloth in the bottom. He wrapped up the book, placed it back in the box, then replaced the lid.

He stepped around the pillar until he came to the back wall. He felt the rocks, trying to feel for the torch handle. He stretched up on his tiptoes, searching for it, but when he did he smelled a strong odor of smoke. He took a deep breath and almost coughed. Smoke? Where in the world did that come from? he wondered. Then he realized—the torch! It must have continued to smolder after it had gone out. Now the whole top of the Vault was filled with smoke.

Stewart whirled around to the door in horror. From the way the light at the top of the door wavered and changed in intensity, he could see that the smoke was escaping the Vault, seeping out the top of the door. At that moment came a shout.

"Fire! Fire in the Vault!"

It was the voice of the Defender who was guarding the door. Stewart pressed himself against the back wall and huddled down. But there was no escape. The door burst open and the Defender rushed in. Stewart defensively raised his hands, but the grab didn't come.

Instead, the Defender wrapped his arms around the stone vessel and ran back outside.

Of course! The Defender had no idea Stewart was in there and would naturally try to save the *Comlat* before doing anything else. Perhaps the Defender would rush the stone vessel to the Curia. This was his chance to escape.

Stewart jumped to his feet and started for the door. But before he managed to get past the pillar, a huge form filled the doorway with a bucket in hand. The next thing he knew, he was hit full force by a blast of cold water. The splash was a shock, but not nearly half as strong as the shock of realization that he had been caught.

CHAPTER 19

Stewart sat in a room of the Curia that contained a table, stools, and, in one corner, a holding cell made of sturdy branches lashed together with vines, like a large primitive cage. His hands were bound behind his back and each ankle was tied to a leg of the stool he was sitting on. He dared not shift his weight for fear of falling over. He sat as still as he could, trying to contain his fear, and watched as the Princeps, who stood on the other side of the room, paged through the *Comlat*.

Lester stood with four other Defenders. His face was red and he was breathing rapidly. His eyes had a wild look and darted from side to side. His whole body was tense. Stewart remembered, when he had first arrived and been brought to the Curia, that Lester had insisted that the Third Prophecy predicted their doom. Stewart realized that, more than anything, Lester was afraid.

The Princeps finally turned the last page of the *Comlat* and closed the book.

"It's all here," she said. "No pages missing, no damage to the text."

"But that doesn't change the fact that they broke the First Law!" Lester shouted.

"Please try to calm down, Lester," said the Princeps. "We'll get to the bottom of this."

A sound of struggle growing louder came from the hallway. "Let me go!" came a familiar voice. A moment later, Cora, looking terrified and held firmly by a Defender, was pushed into the room.

"Sit," the Princeps said to Cora.

The Defender forced Cora down onto a stool next to Stewart and tied her ankles to the stool legs. Her breathing was rapid and shallow. Her already pale face was completely devoid of color.

Seeing how frightened she was made Stewart feel even worse. He had been so sure of the plan that he didn't imagine they would get caught. And he had been so certain that he would find the answer that even if they did get caught it wouldn't have mattered. And now, with no answer and facing exile, he wondered how he could have been so stupid to take such a risk. For both of them. He had to do something.

"It's not her fault," Stewart croaked, his voice barely louder than a whisper. His mouth was dry and he found it difficult to get any sound out. "I made her—"

"Silence," the Princeps said.

Lester jumped forward. "Let the traitor confess!" he protested.

"I said *silence!*" the Princeps said sharply. She paused for a moment and took a deep breath. "Please, everyone be silent, I need to think," she said more softly.

After about a minute, the Princeps turned to Stewart.

"When you went into the Vault, you broke the First Law. Did Cora or anyone else inform you of the First Law and its consequences before you went into the Vault?"

"Yes," Stewart managed to croak, lowering his eyes to stare at the table.

"And still you went in," she said.

"Yes," Stewart said.

"Why?" she asked.

Stewart was so frightened, his voice so tight, that he didn't think he could manage a full explanation. "I already told you," he said, his voice cracking.

"To figure out how the Forebears defeated the Venators and where they went," the Princeps said.

"Yes," Stewart whispered, not looking up.

"And what did you find out?" she asked.

Stewart shook his head.

"Nothing?" she asked.

The way she asked made Stewart look up; did he detect a hint of hope in her voice?

"Did you see all the pages?" she asked.

"Wait a second," Lester said. "Where is this line of questioning going?"

"Let me speak," the Princeps snapped. "You know as well as I do the gravity of the situation, the law broken and the consequences. Before I pass judgment, I need to be certain of the details, all of them."

"Suit yourself," Lester said. "But I heard him confess as clearly as anyone. I don't see the need—"

The Princeps shot Lester a look that made him go silent. She turned back to Stewart.

"So you saw this page?" she asked, holding up the *Comlat* and opening it to the last page, the one containing the Third Prophecy.

Stewart glanced up at the words and the line slashed on the page. He lowered his eyes and nodded.

"And you didn't come up with an answer?"

"No," Stewart said.

The Princeps nodded slowly and closed the book. She looked from Stewart to Cora, then down at the ground. She opened her mouth as though to say something, then closed it. For what felt like an eternity, the room was silent, all eyes on the Princeps. Finally, she raised her head.

"You leave me no choice," the Princeps said. "Cora and Stewart, your actions have put all citizens in grave danger. You have broken the First Law, our most important law, enacted to ensure our survival. Therefore, by the power given to me by the citizens of Bitopia, I hereby sentence you, Cora, and you, Stewart, to exile."

"No!" Cora howled.

"I'm sorry," the Princeps said.

Stewart felt a sensation of cold shoot through his body, as though his insides had turned to ice water and pooled down at his feet.

"Come with me, traitors," Lester said.

He untied their ankles, hauled them roughly to their feet, and started dragging them toward the door, the other Defenders following.

Stewart found it hard to breathe. This can't be happening, he thought. Within minutes they would be outside the wall. As a Gatherer, Cora might know where to go and how to survive, but would she let him come with her? He knew nothing of the land, or how to evade

Venators, or how to move silently. She wouldn't want him along. So where would he go? He had to find someplace safe. But where? Images of the landscape of Bitopia, which he had taken in from the top of the wall, flashed through his mind. Forests, fields, the mountains. He could run, or perhaps Cora would at least row him to safety up the river. The river...

"Wait!" Stewart shouted, digging his heels in the floor, and for a moment, slowing.

Lester, who was much bigger and stronger, shoved Stewart, causing him to stumble forward.

"Princeps!" Stewart shouted. "I figured out the answer in the *Comlat!*"

They were being pushed through the door.

"Princeps!" Stewart howled.

They were out in the hallway.

"Halt!" Stewart heard the Princeps yell.

Lester and his entourage of Defenders stopped.

"Bring them back in here," the Princeps said.

Lester didn't move. "You've rendered judgment," he shouted from the hallway.

"Lester," the Princeps said sternly.

"A judgment rendered is a judgment made," Lester called out.

"This is important, Lester, not for them but for the rest of us," the Princeps said. "If they've figured out something that can help us, we need to know. I'm ordering you to bring them to me."

For a moment, Stewart wasn't sure if Lester would obey. Then he turned them around and pushed them back into the room. For a moment, the Princeps studied Stewart's face, as though trying to discern the honesty of his intent.

"What is it?" the Princeps asked finally.

"It's on the last page of the *Comlat*," Stewart said.

The Princeps opened the book and held it out for him to see. Stewart stared a moment to be certain he was right. That line, the slash with the hook on the end. The view, from the top of the wall, of the river upstream, which meandered, then hooked.

"That line on the page," Stewart said. "It's identical to the path of the river."

The Princeps turned the book around and studied the line.

"From the top of the wall," Stewart said, his voice gaining strength. "That's the path of the river. Cora, don't you think so?"

"He's right," Cora said.

Lester came around them to look closely at the book. "That's just a scratch on the page. A slip of the writing stick. That's nothing."

"And there's a dot there," Stewart said. "Right up by the hook. That could mean something. That could be a map."

The Princeps looked more closely at the page. "That dot, it does look intentional."

"Wait a second," Lester said. "You're not actually buying into this, are you? They're desperate! They'll say anything! Maps have labels! If that's a map, why aren't there any words on it?"

The Princeps ignored him. "Cora, look at this. If this is a map, what is there, at that dot?"

Cora stared at the dot, then slowly shook her head. "I don't know. I haven't been out that way in dozens of harvests."

"Think!" the Princeps commanded.

Stewart realized, from the way the Princeps spoke, that she wanted them to find something. She, too, hoped for an answer.

"I...I...I don't know, I'm sorry!" Cora hung her head and started to cry.

"That's okay, Cora." The Princeps turned to one of the Defenders. "Go fetch as many Gatherers as you can round up and bring them here. I want to know what's at that location."

Stewart felt a growing hope. He had been right! They might not be exiled after all.

"Halt!" Lester said to the Defender who had turned to leave. "Princeps," Lester said, his eyes wild. "The Venators are pounding on the gate. We need as many citizens as we can to help maintain the defenses. I cannot authorize the release of any citizens for non-defensive duties."

"But we may have an answer here," the Princeps said, her anger thinly veiled. "There might be something out there that can help us."

"So what are you going to do?" Lester asked. "Just send out a force to some remote part of Bitopia on the off-chance that some scribble in the *Comlat* is going to save us? You'll have to leave one of the ports open, practically inviting Venators inside! We cannot for a second compromise our defenses. First rule of the Third Prophecy planning. An expedition like this has to be carefully thought through and planned."

After a few moments, the Princeps nodded. "Fine. We'll plan it out, carefully." She gestured to the wooden cage. "In the meantime, put Stewart and Cora in the holding cell."

"The holding cell?" Lester asked. "Oh no, Princeps. You've already rendered judgment. Out they go."

"They may have found something important," the Princeps said. "They deserve to stay until we figure out the meaning of the map."

"There are no mitigating circumstances when it comes to the First Law," Lester said. "You know that. As the law states, nothing could possibly excuse putting the *Comlat* at risk. Immediate exile."

"But he's a Newcomer," the Princeps said to Lester. "He has no survival skills."

From the hint of pleading in her voice, Stewart suddenly realized that they weren't saved after all.

"The law doesn't distinguish when it comes to those who might undermine our ability to survive," Lester said. "I fully expect for you to apply the law fairly and expediently. That is, after all, what we citizens expect of you. As you yourself have said, a judge who no longer fairly applies the law is a judge no longer."

The Princeps swallowed. Lester had put her in a position from which she couldn't back down. She looked at the faces of the other Defenders, who stared back, waiting to see what she would do.

"Return the *Comlat* to the Vault," she ordered two of the Defenders. "And post two guards outside for the time being." She turned to Stewart and Cora, then looked away. "Take them," the Princeps said quietly to the other two Defenders.

"No!" Cora screamed.

Stewart felt himself begin to shake.

Lester tightened his grip on Stewart's arm and opened his mouth to say something, but the Princeps cut him off. "Lester, please return to the gate and continue with the defensive operations." She turned to the two Defenders she had ordered to take Stewart and Cora. "Follow me," she said.

The two Defenders pushed Stewart and Cora along after the Princeps. They left the Curia and headed toward the wall. For the first time since he had entered the city, Stewart desperately wanted to stay inside. To stay inside for even a thousand years would have been a better fate than exile. The wall seemed to rise higher as they approached, and Stewart realized that the time it took for them to reach the wall could very well be most of the remaining time that he, most certainly, and Cora, quite possibly, would be alive.

CHAPTER 20

When they reached the base of the wall, the Princeps led the two Defenders, who had Stewart and Cora firmly in their grasp, around the bordering ring road until they got to a port. A large wooden plug had already been pounded into the opening. The port was sealed.

They continued on and came to the Food Store. Inside, citizens were busy packing food baskets. They looked up and paused when the Princeps entered but then quickly returned to work. When they entered the room with the port, they found that that port, too, had been sealed. Stewart felt his hope rising. He looked at Cora who was thinking the same thing. If all the ports were sealed, there would be no way to get out. They would be forced to stay inside until the battle was over.

At the third port, one that was on the opposite side of the city from the gate, their hopes came crashing down. A large wooden plug, like a tapered cork with a long pointed spike protruding from the end, stood a few feet from the opening, against which rested two enormous wooden mallets. Two Defenders, with sharpened poles in their hands, stood next to the porthole.

"Why is this port open?" the Princeps demanded. She, too, appeared to be surprised.

"Still waiting for Benjamin," one of the Defenders said.

At that moment, the rope that passed through the porthole went taut. The Defenders quickly crouched down, holding their pointed sticks forward. They peered into the hole. One of the Defenders then dropped his pole and reached into the port. A moment later, a boy came sliding through, pulled by the Defender. His nose was bloody and his hands were cut up. When he popped out and onto the ground, he lay doubled over, moaning. Stewart stared in horror. That would be his own fate, he realized, for the rest of his short life.

"Quick," the Princeps said to the Defenders holding Stewart and Cora. "Get Benjamin to the Infirmary."

They hesitated, still holding onto Stewart and Cora.

"We'll handle it," the Princeps said, indicating the other two Defenders who were guarding the door. "Go, now!"

The Defenders released Stewart and Cora and gently picked up the boy. He groaned and managed to hobble off, supported by the Defenders. As soon as they were out of earshot, the Princeps pulled Stewart and Cora close.

"Now listen to me," she said as she started to unbind their hands. "Ever since our discussion in my office, I've been thinking about what you said. And the more I thought about it, the more I think, Stewart, that you might be right. The Forebears must have won. I'm sorry I didn't believe you at first, but I think you can understand."

Stewart nodded.

"I believe," the Princeps continued, "that you've found something in the *Comlat* that can help us defeat the Venators. Go now as fast as you can to the spot indicated on the map and find it. I'll keep this port open as long as possible."

Stewart's joy at the Princeps' admission was quickly tempered by a vision of the battered and bloody Benjamin.

"If you believe me," Stewart asked, "why are you exiling us?"

The Princeps' face softened. "Even if you hadn't broken the First Law, I would still ask you to go." She took a deep breath. "The gate is not going to hold. We never expected this tactic."

Cora's eyes grew wide. The Princeps nodded.

"You are far safer getting out now," she continued, "than waiting around here. If you come back and see that the gate has been breached, run and hide in the forest riverfront. All the citizens will gather there. If, for whatever reason, your lives are in danger, use whatever it is you've found to save yourselves."

The Princeps turned to Cora and put her hands on her shoulders. "I'm so glad it is you who found Stewart and got mixed up in all this. Of all the Gatherers, you've got the speed and skills to survive out there. Be brave. I know you can do this. And take good care of Stewart. Now go, quickly!"

To Stewart's surprise, Cora didn't protest but turned and crawled into the port. Stewart bent down and took hold of the rope to follow after her. As he pulled himself into the narrow stone tunnel, he heard the Princeps instruct the Defenders guarding the port not to seal it except under her direct orders.

Stewart's head was spinning. He had been right, he had found something in the *Comlat*, he and Cora had been exiled, the Princeps was on their side and taking a risk to protect them, they were about to leave the protective wall of the city that was surrounded by hundreds if not thousands of Venators, and he had no idea if he and Cora would live or die.

And that spot on the page of the *Comlat*. Did it mark the location of some kind of weapon, such as a magical orb, that could drive the Venators away and get them home? And, if they did manage to make it that far, how would they recognize it? What if it was buried in the ground?

Despite all these questions, for the first time in a long time—years, it felt like—the outcome was in his own hands. He had been trapped in the city, trapped behind the wall, but now he was doing something about it. With renewed strength, he pulled on the rope, hauling himself through the port and out into the night.

CHAPTER 21

Stewart slid out from the porthole and crouched down next to Cora. His heart was pounding. He expected that at any moment a group of Venators would jump them. They both remained motionless, listening. Every now and then, they would hear the pounding footsteps of a Venator rushing past the grove of trees in which they were hidden. But beyond that, the only sound was that of the pounding on the front gate. The sound was muted, distant, as they were on the opposite side of the city from the gate.

Cora motioned to Stewart to follow and they crept through the underbrush to the scritchy bushes that ringed the grove. For a long time, Cora peered through the branches, looking for any sign of movement. Then, very slowly, she raised herself up until she could just see over the branches and out into the plain to their left, the forest in front of them, and the field of thicker undergrowth to their right. She was like a cat, Stewart thought, patient and certain in her movements, skills she must have developed during decades of working as a Gatherer. After what felt like an eternity, she lowered herself back down and put her mouth right up to Stewart's ear.

"No matter what," she whispered in the quietest voice Stewart had ever heard, "we cannot be seen or heard. With all the Venators around, we'd never escape." She stopped and listened, then continued. "We need to get to the boat. I can row faster than the Venators can swim, so if we can make it there we have a good chance of getting away." She paused to listen. "Follow me, do as I do, and don't make a sound."

She looked Stewart in the eyes, giving him an intense stare. He suddenly realized that not only had he gotten her exiled, but he was now a burden to her as well. She could probably make it on her own with her years of experience moving about Bitopia and evading the Venators, but the Princeps had made him her responsibility. He owed her big time.

Cora scanned ahead, then very slowly grabbed a scritchy branch and moved it aside. She slipped through and moved to the next one. Stewart followed. Halfway through, a thorn from a branch caught on his pants. He didn't see it in the darkness and when he kept moving forward, the branch pulled, then snapped back, rustling the bushes. Cora immediately dropped down into a crouch and shot him a look to be more careful. Stewart silently cursed himself for his clumsiness.

When they emerged at the very edge of the grove, they sat in a crouch for a number of minutes, watching and listening. Finally, Cora tugged on his sleeve and took off running toward a bush two dozen feet away. Stewart didn't know if he was supposed to run right behind her or wait until she made it. So he waited. And then he heard the footsteps.

They sounded like an approaching herd of galloping horses, rhythmic and pounding. The sound grew louder, and Stewart sat, unable to move, fear welling up inside. He couldn't run across to the bush, as then he would be seen. And he couldn't back up fast enough through the scritchy branches without making noise. He was going to be caught. He was going to be beaten by a gang of Venators. He was going to die.

He looked across at Cora. She was pointing her finger rapidly at the ground, then started rocking wildly, forward and backward, rearing up then bowing her head. The footsteps grew louder. From the way the sound changed, Stewart realized that the Venators had rounded the wall and were in view.

Stewart was still sheltered by a few scritchy bushes, but at any moment the Venators would spot him, sitting helplessly on the ground. He wanted to scream but he found he couldn't breathe. He looked over at Cora, but she had disappeared. Had she run? Then he realized where she had gone. She was still there, but was facedown against the ground. Her pale skin, which shone like a beacon, was no longer visible. Her dark and drab clothing made her nearly invisible. That's what she was trying to tell him with her rocking.

Stewart saw movement out of the corner of his eye. The Venators. They were almost upon him. Fighting every instinct that suddenly and fiercely flared—to run, to fight, to stare at the grotesque creatures—Stewart tucked his arms under his chest and drove his face right down into the dirt so only his clothes would be visible. The pounding of their feet grew louder and louder until Stewart was certain they would run right over his head.

And then they were past him, the sound fading into the night as they ran around the city wall. Stewart slowly raised his head, then jumped, startled. Cora was crouched right next to him. He hadn't even heard her approach. Without a word, she grabbed his arm and pulled him across the open ground to the bush.

"When I said to follow me, I meant stay right behind me," she whispered. "When I move, you move. Come on."

They made their way from bush to bush, across the plain, following the reverse route they had taken the day Stewart had arrived in Bitopia. In the light of the pink and yellow moons, the colorful leaves of the bushes and trees took on a pastel appearance, as though he were moving about in an old hand-colored postcard.

Halfway between the city and the river, they were able to see the front gate. There were hundreds of Venators gathered around, most of them moving about beyond the ring of bonfires. From a distance, they appeared as a shifting mass of arms and legs, gangly and grotesque, wrapped in bands of shadow and flickering firelight.

The Venators had taken a break from their pounding, and the ram had been pulled back from the wall, out of range of anything the citizens might throw to try to damage it. The Venators were busy finishing the ram tunnel, throwing buckets of what appeared to be mud on the roof. Every now and then, Stewart spied something thrown from the wall—a stone, a flaming stick, a hunk of wood. The Venators wielding the wooden shields easily deflected the thrown objects.

The Venators were apparently putting all their efforts into getting through the front gate. The only thing standing between them and entry into the city was time, the time it would take for the stone ram point to get through the wooden doors and the crossbeams behind them. And that was all the time that Stewart and Cora had to find the object the Forebears had hidden and get back to the city. With the ram-wielders taking a break, the countdown clock had stopped temporarily, but soon the ticking would start again with each strike of the ram, the bits of wood from the gate like the grains of sand draining into the bottom of an hourglass.

Cora tugged on Stewart's sleeve and they pushed on toward the river. Walking grew more difficult as they were crossing the path that the invading Venator force used to approach the city. The ground was chewed up from hundreds of feet and dozens of wagon wheels, the grass pounded into the rutted and muddy earth.

They finally reached the trees that lined the bank of the river and peered around to ensure that no Venators were down at the water, filling their buckets. When they stepped down toward the river, Stewart felt a twinge of relief; they were now out of sight of the city and the Venators surrounding the gate. With the Venators massed around the city, perhaps their chances of running into them farther away from the city were diminished. Perhaps they would be free to find whatever it was the map indicated with no interference. Perhaps...

The close proximity of a guttural shout sent a shock down Stewart's spine. Stewart and Cora whirled around in the direction of the sound, a low howl that sounded like a cross between the growl of a rabid dog and the snort of an enraged bull. Farther down the bank, in the black shadows cast by the trees, they saw movement. Venators. They had been spotted.

Cora grabbed his arm and pulled him hard in the opposite direction, breaking the paralysis caused by his fear and shock. They dug their toes into the soft earth, accelerating into a sprint up the riverbank. They plunged into the bush where Cora had hidden the boat, Stewart ramming his knee into the hull. Oblivious to the pain, he grabbed the side and helped drag the boat toward the water.

As they reached the water's edge, the Venators emerged from the shadows of the trees and into the moonslight. They were running full tilt, their long sinewy legs covering half a dozen feet per stride. Their eyes were deep-set and black, almost devoid of light, like two circles of pure emptiness. And their mouths—yellowed teeth, lips so thin they were almost nonexistent—were twisted into expressions of joyful rage.

The next thing Stewart knew, something hit him on his shoulder, knocking him off balance, and the stars in the sky and twin moons floated across his vision. Then his head cracked into something hard and for a moment everything was dark and silent. A split second later he felt his whole body jerk. His legs, which had been up in the air, came down and he sat up. He was in the stern of the boat, which Cora had just pushed out into the water. He realized that she had shoved him in.

The Venators were closing, and fast. Cora leapt from the bank, over Stewart, and landed on the middle seat of the boat. She dropped the oar blades into the water and began to row furiously. They pulled away from shore, slowly, then faster.

The Venator in the lead reached the water's edge.

Cora pulled hard on the oars, causing the boat to surge with each stroke.

The Venator splashed into the shallows.

Cora pulled with all her might.

The Venator jumped, arms extended.

Cora yanked hard on one oar, trying to spin the stern away.

One calloused, bony hand managed to grab the edge of the boat.

Cora screamed.

CHAPTER 22

The weight of the Venator grabbing onto the back of the boat caused the whole craft to dip down toward the stern, the bow rising into the air. The sudden jerk of the boat caused Stewart to fall onto his back again. The Venator's hand was inches from Stewart's feet.

In a sheer panic, Stewart struggled to both get upright and get away from the Venator. He kicked with his feet, trying to push against something, anything. He kicked against the stern, then his foot missed and shot over the edge of the boat. The Venator grabbed it with its free hand. Stewart yanked it away, out of the Venator's grasp. He kicked again, but the Venator had pulled itself closer to the boat. The creature reached over the edge and grabbed Stewart's ankle in a vice-like bony grip.

The strength of the Venator's grip was frightening. Stewart, who had one foot braced against the stern, tried to push himself away and break the Venator's hold, but to no avail. The Venator started to pull. Stewart looked up in desperation at Cora, but she was standing on the seat, an oar in hand, swinging the blade over the water, trying to keep the other Venators off the outriggers.

The Venator pulled and Stewart slid closer. Stewart pushed as hard as he could, but he couldn't match the strength of the Venator. He could see the creature's face and shoulders just above the edge of the boat. He grabbed onto the seat, but it was no help.

Stewart realized that there was only one thing left to do, one action that, if it failed, it would mean certain doom. Stewart gripped the seat with all his might and pulled back the foot that was braced against the stern.

The yank that pulled him straight toward the Venator was so hard that for a moment Stewart wondered if his leg had been ripped from his hip socket. But that additional force was exactly what Stewart needed. With a howl of his own, Stewart drove the heel of his free foot *smack* into the Venator's nose.

The Venator shrieked, a high-pitch whine of pain. It released Stewart's ankle and brought both hands to its face. Dark red blood, almost black, started flowing between the Venator's fingers. The other Venators, who were trying to get past Cora's swinging oar, stopped in surprise.

But Cora didn't. In a flash, she dropped onto her seat, returned the oar to the oarlock, and pulled hard. The boat shot out into the middle of the river. The Venators, now over their surprise, howled in anger. But they didn't follow, as the boat was now out of reach. Cora rowed hard and without a break until the Venators were far behind them, the city out of sight, the smoke from the fires just a dark smudge on the distant sky.

CHAPTER 23

For the better part of two hours, Cora and Stewart followed the river upstream, the only sound the rhythmic splashing of the oars, the creak of the oarlocks, and various bugs and beetles singing and humming in the night. Finally, Cora stopped rowing and let the boat drift.

"I need a rest," she said. She stretched her arms, then rolled her head from side to side to relax her neck. "That was very brave, what you did back there," she said. "No one has ever done that to a Venator before, at least that I know of."

"I had no choice," Stewart said.

"Still," Cora said. "You saved us back there. Thank you."

"You saved me twice so far," Stewart said, "so I still owe you one."

"Fair enough," she said.

She sat with her arms resting on her legs, the oars held loosely in her hands. Stewart wondered what they were waiting for, then realized that she must be really tired.

"You want me to row?" Stewart asked.

"Do you know how?" she asked.

Stewart shook his head. "But you might as well teach me," he said. "Who knows how long we'll be out here. And if you should get hurt, you'll need me to row anyway."

"Good point," she said.

They switched places and Cora told Stewart how to sit, centered on the seat with his feet braced on the bottom of the boat. He took the oars in his hands and Cora instructed him on how to swing them back, catch the blades on the water, then pull first with his torso, then his arms and shoulders.

Stewart gave it a try. It took a few practice swings to catch the oars at the same time. The first few times he did it, the oar blades dropped deeply into the water, and once the oar got yanked out of his hand. But after a few more tries Stewart got the hang of it. Soon he was powering the boat up the river. He felt a little disconcerted at first, as he was sitting with his back to the direction they were going, and he had never driven anything facing backward. He was afraid that he would row them right into the bank, but he soon learned how to judge their position on the river just by seeing the banks on either side in his peripheral vision, with an occasional glance over his shoulder to confirm their heading.

The moons continued on their paths across the sky, the smaller yellow one moving closer and closer to the larger pink one before moving in front of it, creating a yellow disk ringed with a pink fringe. They rowed in silence, the river meandering but not yet hooking sharply to the left, the landmark they needed to find. After a while, Cora insisted on switching even though Stewart's arms were not yet fully tired; she said it was better to alternate and rest than get completely worn out.

They hadn't seen any Venators, which Cora said was a very good sign. They must, she theorized, be all around the city. Stewart relaxed a bit, feeling at least marginally safe.

Stewart was sitting in the back of the boat, with a view of the river ahead of him, when he saw a dark line ahead of them on the water. As they got closer, he saw it was the riverbank, shrouded in the shadow of trees. They were coming to the sharp turn.

"What now?" Stewart asked after they had rounded the bend.

"Your guess is as good as mine," she said.

Maybe they would see it when they came to it, Stewart thought. He pictured the line and dot as written on the last page of the *Comlat*. Had the map been to scale? How would they know how far to go upstream, and how far to go inland to find the place marked by the dot?

Stewart studied the bank on the right side of the boat, looking for some sign that they had gone far enough. Bushes, yellow in color, grew thickly along both banks right at the edge of the water and grew denser the farther upstream they went. But there was no sign of anything out of the ordinary that would indicate the spot they were trying to reach. Cora also kept looking over her shoulder as well but apparently didn't see anything, either, as she didn't slow the pace of her strokes.

They heard the sound long before they saw it, a low roar of water crashing over rocks. Ahead of them, the river had turned white, foaming and frothing. When they got close, they saw that rapids, with large rocks jutting out of the water, spanned the full width of the river. As they had been heading toward the mountains, it was only natural that the gradient of the river would increase, the water flowing faster over the steeper rocky sections. But there was no way the boat could get through the rapids.

Cora rowed over to the bank to get out of the swift current. They sat in an eddy, the rotating flow of water gently carrying the boat in a slow circle.

"Do you think this is where we get out?" Stewart asked. "The Forebears certainly couldn't have made it past this point."

"We have to go back," Cora said. She pointed to the yellow bushes lining the shore. "We call those snag bushes. No chance getting through those."

Stewart looked more closely at the bushes when the eddy brought them near the shore. Under the covering of yellow leaves, he saw that the branches were covered with long, pointed thorns. Trying to push through would be like plowing into a pile of porcupines.

"But where we want to go must be on the other side of the bushes," Stewart said. "The snag bushes started growing along the bank all the way back at the bend. And it could be harder going on foot. We could run into a whole grove of snag bushes."

"What other choice do we have?" Cora asked. "There's no way to cut through—"

"Shhh!" Stewart said, cutting her off. "Look!" he whispered.

On the bank halfway up the rapids, a creature had appeared. It was like a deer, but smaller, with a single horn that grew from the middle of its head. The horn branched out into an antler, half a dozen delicate points on each side. The creature stepped to the edge of the water, dipped its head, and drank.

Stewart and Cora sat watching, not daring to make a sound. But then the eddy pulled the boat farther out into the river and the creature raised its head. It stared at them for a moment, then turned and was gone.

"That was a unideer," Cora said. "We gave it that name because of the single antler. Come on," she said, "let's go back."

"Wait!" Stewart said. "Don't you see? The unideer drank from the river!"

"So?" Cora said.

"There must be a gap in the bushes," Stewart said, excited. "If the unideer got through, we should be able to as well."

"But how are we going to get there?" she asked. "It's up the rapids!"

Stewart studied the river. A powerful current cut down the middle, smashing into rocks the size of hippos. But the current on the sides of the rapids was not so strong. And although there were foamy holes and whirlpools, they were small.

"We'll wade through the water along the side," Stewart said.

"No!" Cora said. "We can't do that!"

"Why not?" Stewart asked. "It's not that far. And the water isn't deep."

"I can't," Cora said.

"Why?" Stewart asked.

"Because," Cora said quietly. "I can't swim."

"You never learned how?" Stewart asked.

"I've been kind of busy the last few decades," Cora snapped.

"Sorry," Stewart said. "But we won't be swimming, we'll be walking. Come on, it's not that far, not too deep, and the current isn't that fast."

Cora looked fearfully at the rapids. Reluctantly, she nodded. She backed the boat up and then pulled hard on the oars, sending the boat surging toward the bank. The bow of the boat shot straight into the snag bushes, making a grating sound as the whole front half got lodged securely into the thorny branches.

Stewart swung his feet over the edge of the boat and slipped down into the water. It was cool but not unpleasant. The bottom was covered with smooth stones, but the rocks were covered with either mud or slime as his feet had a hard time keeping their grip.

"Careful," he said. "The bottom is slippery."

Cora moved toward the stern, then slowly put one foot over the edge. She dipped down into the water next to Stewart, her eyes growing wide as she sank to her neck. She held the side of the boat so tightly her knuckles were white. They carefully made their way around the outrigger and approached the bottom of the rapids.

Stewart went into the rough water first, feeling the bottom carefully with his feet. The water was waist deep, and the power of the current was much stronger than he expected. For a moment, he considered turning around and following Cora's suggestion of going back to the bend, but the gap in the bushes was in sight.

Stewart came to a place where the current ran between the shore and a foamy hole. The water flowed over and around a large rock and formed a bubbly depression, the water circulating around and around, like a sideways whirlpool. He did not like the look of it one bit.

"Give me your arm," Stewart yelled over the roar of the water, reaching back to Cora.

"I'm fine," she said.

"It'll be safer," Stewart said.

"I don't need your help," Cora snapped.

Stewart knew she felt embarrassed to have admitted her fear of the water, and he wanted to tell her that it was okay, it didn't matter. But he knew that she wasn't going to listen.

"Well then, just be careful," he said.

He pushed his way farther along, the effort to just lift a leg and push it upstream draining. A few times he lost his footing and almost instinctively grabbed onto a snag bush branch, but he managed to right himself. He was getting closer to the gap. Just a few more steps.

Stewart heard a scream that was suddenly cut off by a splash. He turned around. Cora was gone.

"Cora!" he shouted.

Stewart scanned the water looking for some sign of her, hoping at any moment that she would pop up next to the boat. He took a few steps downstream until he was next to the foamy hole. And that's when he saw her.

Cora was trapped underwater, rising to the surface, then plunging down again, then coming up and going back down. But she couldn't break the surface. And that meant she couldn't get air. She was going to drown.

Stewart frantically scanned the nearby bank, looking for a long branch to use to pull her out. He thought of using his belt, but it wasn't long enough. He could tie his shirt to his belt. But he was running out of time.

He knew that trying to rescue a drowning person usually resulted in two drowning deaths, the person drowning and the rescuer, and that only trained and skilled people should ever attempt a rescue. But she needed his help and there was no one else around. And without Cora, he wasn't going to survive out in the Bitopian wilderness. He waited until she rose close to the surface again, then he took a deep breath and dove into the hole.

CHAPTER 24

The instant Stewart plunged in, he knew he was in trouble. The power of the rotating water was overwhelming. There was nothing he could do to counteract its force. He was completely in its grasp. But yet, strangely, he felt calm. He had made a choice to either succeed or die, so he knew exactly what he faced.

He could tell when the circulating water thrust him toward the surface as the greenish black water brightened momentarily before he was once again pulled toward the bottom of the hole and enveloped in darkness. Near the surface, the water was filled with millions of bubbles, and his hands and legs kicked and cut right through the aerated water, preventing him from breaking the surface and getting air. But when he plunged down to the bottom of the hole, the water was denser, like in a swimming pool. And at the very bottom of each loop, he could feel a slight downstream pull before being shot up to the surface again. He realized that water going into the hole had to exit somehow, and it must be leaving from the bottom. The only way out was to do the exact opposite of what any drowning person would want to do: swim down.

His lungs were hurting and now he started to panic. If he didn't get out, he was going to die. He felt something, as he swirled around and around, bumping against his leg, and grabbed onto it. It was soft and struggling. Cora.

The pressure in his chest was building. Cora, of course, from all her decades of running, undoubtedly had a bigger lung capacity, which is probably why she was still alive. But neither of them would be much longer. He knew they only had one chance to escape.

As they dropped down into the hole, the water getting darker and more substantial, Stewart, holding one arm around Cora, kicked as hard as he could with his feet down toward the bottom. With his free hand he pulled strokes, trying to break out of the vertical whirlpool. He felt the speed of the rotating current slow, then he bumped into a rock on the bottom of the river. Then another. Desperate, he grasped onto it and pulled.

For a moment, they didn't move. They were suspended in the water, held by the tug-of-war between the upward-rushing hydraulic and the downstream flow. Then they started moving slowly toward the rock. And then, in a sudden rush, they accelerated down the river. They were free.

Like an erupting geyser, they both shot to the surface, gasping for breath, arms flailing, coughing on the inhaled spray and splashing. Holding onto each other, they bumped and banged their way down the rapids until they were spat out into the calm waters at the bottom. Stewart kept a firm grasp on Cora and swam her out of the current and into the eddy. He pulled her to the stern of the boat and helped her grab onto the edge. For a long time, they hung onto the back of the boat, both of them breathing heavily.

"I swear," Cora said at last, "that if I ever get home, I'm going to learn how to swim."

Stewart laughed, more a nervous release of energy than anything.

"And thank you," Cora said. "You saved my life."

"Now we're even," Stewart said.

Cora laughed. "I guess you're right."

"Let's get into the boat," Stewart said. "We'll go back to the bend."

"No," Cora said. "No. We're going back up the rapids. And this time I won't be so stubborn."

"You don't have to do this," Stewart said, still frightened by what they just endured. "I'm sure we can make it through on land."

"We're going back up the rapids," Cora said. "The best thing to do when you fear something is to face it. If I run away now, I know I'll never go near water again. Come on."

They made their way back up the bank, Stewart leading again, but this time they held onto each other, firmly grasping each other's wrists. They agreed that they would alternate taking steps so that one of them would always be on firm footing while the other moved. Stewart led them as close to the bank as possible as they passed the hole, and a couple of times he got scratched by the snag bushes when he brushed the branches. Twice Cora slipped, and once Stewart lost his footing, but neither went under.

At last they reached the gap where the unideer had appeared. A narrow path led between the snag bushes and up the muddy bank. They stood for a moment in the water, searching for signs of movement, or any other indication that Venators awaited them. But everything was still, and the only sound was that of the river. Warily, they climbed onto the bank and moved into the cover of the undergrowth.

CHAPTER 25

The track they followed was narrow and wound through a grove of snag bushes, small trees, and tall grasses. They crept through the darkness, Cora leading. Stewart realized they were following an animal trail, worn by all the animals in that area that converged on the river for a drink. As they walked away from the river, the trail grew less distinct as the separation in the undergrowth allowed creatures to reach the trail from many directions. Soon they found themselves swishing through the grasses carpeting a sparse forest.

They were in the Outer Reaches, close to the foot of the mountains. Moonslight reflected off the snowfields blanketing the peaks, the snow in the darkness appearing almost blue. A breeze of heavy, cool air washed down from the slopes, making Cora and Stewart shiver slightly in their wet clothes. On both sides, the land rose up gradually, and soon they found themselves walking into a low valley.

Stewart had no idea if they were heading in the right direction, and for a moment he was struck by a fear that the quest was hopeless. It was one thing to follow a river, as they couldn't go off track. But they were trying to find a spot marked on a map by a dot on a page with no guidance on the distance or heading. There were an infinite number of directions that they could go, and only one was the right one. And, if by chance they were heading in the right direction, how would they know when they got there? What if whatever the Forebears had used to defeat the Venators was buried and the spot wasn't marked? And if it were, how would they dig it up? And what if they found something that they didn't know how to use?

Stewart pushed those thoughts out of his mind. While there was a greater chance that they were on the wrong track, there was still a chance they were heading in the right direction. And since they were meant to find whatever it was they were looking for, the Forebears would certainly make sure it could be found. Otherwise, they would likely have provided more information in the *Comlat*.

They trudged through the scrub, Cora's head constantly turning from side to side, a habit, Stewart guessed, that came from Gathering. He scanned too, but instead of looking for Venators, he focused on what might be different in the landscape, something out of the ordinary, such as a rock pile to mark a spot or a tree with information carved into the bark.

The ridges grew steeper on either side of them and the valley floor began to slope upward. They had to pick their way around trees and bushes as they climbed. The ridgelines were converging and soon they would reach the top. At the very least, the top might offer a vantage point from which to survey their surroundings.

The undergrowth abruptly gave way to a small clearing. Across the clearing, where the hill they were climbing rose sharply, was an outcropping of blue-gray rock. Underneath a low and wide ledge of the outcropping was an oval-shaped opening, the mouth of a cave.

Stewart's heart leapt. Could this be it? The Forebears could very well have hidden the device in a cave to protect it from the weather. If they had the foresight to build the Vault to protect the *Comlat*, they certainly would have taken great care to protect whatever object could save the next generation from the Venators. If this was in fact that spot on the map, all they would have to do was go in, retrieve it, and get back into the city. He looked at Cora, whose wide eyes and smile indicated she was thinking the same thing. She grabbed his arm and they started running across the clearing.

Movement in the cave mouth brought them to a skidding halt. They both stared into the darkness of the opening, not sure what moved. It was a large, dark mass, not a Venator. Two pinpricks of light became visible as the creature slowly emerged. Stewart wanted to run, but he felt as though his feet had turned to lead. The creature that emerged was a wolf, larger than a man.

The wolf came out of the cave, stretched its back, then sat down. It stared at them, unblinking. Stewart wanted to glance over at Cora, but he was afraid that any sudden movement might cause the animal to leap. And there was no way they would be able to escape a creature of that size. The unexpected sound of Cora's voice made him jump.

"Good evening, great and gentle Wolf," Cora said in a calm voice.

For a moment, Stewart couldn't believe that her voice didn't betray her fear. But then he remembered that the creatures of Bitopia could talk. And she had run into dozens of creatures like this in her decades of Gathering. She might even know this creature.

"Good evening, little one," the wolf replied.

Its voice was low, but soothing. Stewart found the sound to be quite calming.

"My name is Cora, and this is Stewart," she said. "We apologize if we have disturbed you this evening."

"No apology needed," the wolf said. "I had not yet gone to sleep. What brings you little ones out so far from your stone lair?"

"We're seeking something our Forebears hid in this area," she said. "Our city, or stone lair as you call it, came under attack from the Venators, the big spindly creatures that torment us. We believe this thing our Forebears hid can help us defeat the Venators."

"Interesting," the wolf said.

"With your kind permission," Cora said, "we'd like to keep searching."

"Search away," the wolf said. "But what are you looking for, exactly?"

"We don't know," Cora said. "We're hoping that it is obvious. The Forebears drew a map, and what we're searching for is somewhere in this area."

Stewart leaned over and whispered in Cora's ear. "Maybe he has seen something out of the ordinary around here. Ask him."

"What's that, little one?" the wolf asked, his eyes narrowing.

Stewart swallowed. "I...I...just wondered if maybe you know where it is."

The wolf smiled, his long teeth glinting in the moonslight. "There was no need to whisper, little one; you could have just asked me. Tell me—are you frightened of me?"

"He only just got here," Cora said quickly and apologetically. "He hasn't met any of the creatures in this world yet."

"I asked him the question, not you," the wolf said to Cora.

The wolf turned his eyes back on Stewart. For a split second, Stewart felt like running, but he knew he had to stand there and answer.

"Yes," Stewart said in a quiet voice. "I am frightened."

"Why?" asked the wolf.

Stewart blinked, not expecting the question. "Why? Well, you're so big, and you've got huge teeth."

"Because I look different?" the wolf asked.

"No, because you look scary," Stewart said. "I'm sorry, I mean no insult, it's just, well, I don't know, I feel scared."

"The same way you feel scared by the Venators," the wolf said.

"Well, yes," Stewart admitted. "Aren't you frightened of the Venators?"

"Actually, they are frightened by me," the wolf said. "They run when they see me. I don't know why. I mean them no harm, but yet they still run."

"Really?" Stewart asked. "They run away from you? Even groups of them?"

The wolf nodded. Stewart suddenly had an idea.

"Would you help us?" Stewart asked. "Please?"

"How?" the wolf asked. "In what way?"

"If the Venators are frightened of you, you could drive them away from the city," Stewart said. "You could send them all running."

"You're right, I could," the wolf said. He sat for a moment, thinking. "But let me ask you this. If I were to come with you and drive them away, wouldn't they eventually come back and attack again?"

"Well, yes," Stewart said slowly, "but that would give us time to fortify the city and find whatever it was the Forebears hid out here."

"But what if you didn't find it?" the wolf asked.

"Well..." Stewart mulled over the question.

"You would be attacked again and again until the Venators won," the wolf said. "Wouldn't it be better to have a way to defeat the Venators once and for all?"

"Yes, that's exactly what we're looking for," Stewart said. "Some kind of weapon that they hid."

"And what kind of weapon could that possibly be?" the wolf asked.

"I don't know," Stewart said, looking at Cora. "Something powerful, more powerful than the Venators."

"Powerful," the wolf repeated. "Let me ask you something. What is it that makes the Venators more powerful than you?"

"They're big," Stewart said.

"And they beat us up," Cora added.

"They're scary," Stewart said.

"Scary," the wolf said. "Like me."

"No, not like you," Stewart said. "It's just..."

"Didn't you feel like running when you first saw me?" the wolf asked.

"Well, yes," Stewart admitted.

"You were afraid of me," the wolf said. "And that gave me power over you."

"How do you mean?" Stewart asked.

"Let me demonstrate," the wolf said. The wolf let out a low growl and rose in volume until it ended in a ferocious bark. Both Stewart and Cora flinched, but looked at the wolf curiously, wondering why he had done that.

The wolf smiled. "If I had done that when you first approached my cave, you would have fled, wouldn't you?"

Stewart nodded.

"But now, since you know that I mean you no harm, you don't run," the wolf said. "That same growl doesn't have the same power. Not because the growl is any different, but because you are not afraid. And now I don't have the same power over you.

"Let me ask you this," the wolf continued. "What is it that makes you run from the Venators, that gives them such power over you?"

"They're mean and cruel," Cora answered.

"No, that's not it," the wolf said, shaking his head.

"I know," Stewart said. "Our fear."

"Exactly," the wolf replied. "Exactly. Your fear gives them power. And the more you fear them, the more powerful they become."

Neither Stewart nor Cora answered. They hadn't thought of it that way before.

"I didn't make you scared of me, Stewart," the wolf said. "That fear came from within you. But your fear of me gave me power over you. Same with the Venators, for you too, Cora, and all the other little ones. The Venators' power comes not from being able to hurt you but from being able to scare you. Your fear gives power to that which you fear. What if," the wolf asked slowly, "you become less scared of the Venators? Is it possible that they would become less powerful, weak even?"

"But how can you do that, make yourself less scared?" Cora asked.

"There are two ways," the wolf said. "The first is that you can trust in your knowledge that the Venators' power comes from your own fear. Have the Venators ever seriously harmed or killed one of the little ones?"

"No," Cora replied.

"So you see, they just want to scare you. And the more fear you show, by trying to run, for example, the more confident and aggressive they get. But the less you fear them, the less power they have over you. So don't be afraid, as you have nothing to fear."

Stewart tried to imagine not being afraid while surrounded by a dozen Venators.

The wolf read the expressions on their faces and chuckled. "Not the easiest way, is it."

Stewart shook his head. "And the second?"

"The second way, believe it or not, is to act like you are not scared," the wolf said. "Just as I recognized your fear of me when you whispered to your friend, the Venators fully recognize your fear of them. So don't react. Don't let them see how they upset you or bother you. Pretend you are not afraid. Appear calm and confident. The Venators won't know the difference. Be as frightened as you want to be on the inside, but don't show it to them on the outside.

"If you appear to be unafraid, then the Venators will believe you really are unafraid and they will start to lose their power. When you see that they aren't so powerful, you will become more confident and inside you will feel less fear, which will make you appear even more unafraid on the outside. And so the cycle will continue until finally the Venators' power is gone.

"Now I must warn you that they will still torment you at first, and possibly more so, as they won't believe this change that's come over you. But when they finally see you are not scared, not bothered by them, that you don't run, and that you don't get angry or fight back, they will lose interest and go away. I guarantee it."

An image of Josh Johnson, on the playground at school, suddenly flashed in Stewart's mind. Josh was no match physically for Dirk, Frankie, and Judd, but he had stood his ground, and the bullies had gone away. It wasn't what Josh had said to them, but rather his apparent lack of fear. Without fear, the bullies had no power over him.

"They want you to run, to be frightened," the wolf said. "It makes their torments of you so satisfying. But what would happen if you were to stand there, unafraid? Laughing even? If I were you, I would invite them into your stone lair to show them that you are not scared. They will lose their power, and once they do, they lose it forever. They will never attack you again."

"Invite them in?" Cora said, incredulous. "You mean, open the gate?"

"Yes, exactly," the wolf said.

Although the thought of inviting the entire Venator army into the city seemed crazy, what the wolf said made sense, Stewart realized. It would be hard pretending not to be scared, but if all the citizens stuck together, they just might be able to do it.

"Do you understand?" the wolf asked.

Stewart and Cora nodded.

"So you see, you don't need some weapon or a big scary creature to drive the Venators away," the wolf said. "You have the power yourselves. Oh, and one last thing."

"Yes?" asked Stewart.

"You said there was a map in a book that led you to this area?" the wolf asked.

"Yes," Cora said. "A line showing the river, and then a dot."

"When the little ones came to me for help all those years ago, hoping I would chase the Franks away, as they called the Venators, I told the little ones to clearly mark in their book how to find me again in case more little ones came after them and needed help. Please do me a favor and make the directions to my lair more explicit. I can't imagine what would have happened if you had taken a different valley from the river."

Both Cora and Stewart's jaws dropped.

The wolf laughed, a rapid series of gentle barks. "Yes, my lair is the spot on the map. I'm the secret weapon, or rather, the information I just gave you is what you were intended to find."

Stewart and Cora looked at each other. This wasn't what they had been expecting at all. But it made perfect sense.

"Wait a second," Cora said, her anger flaring. "You knew how to defeat the Venators this whole time, for all the years we've been here? Why didn't you tell us?"

"Would you have listened?" the wolf asked.

Cora opened her mouth to reply, then closed it again.

"You were not ready," the wolf said. "The information I have passed to you is only good when you seek it, for only then do you have the courage that you need to use it."

Cora's angry expression turned thoughtful, and she nodded slowly.

"What happened to the Forebears?" Stewart asked.

"Soon after the little ones returned to their stone lair and drove the Venators away, both the little ones and the Venators disappeared," the wolf said.

"The Forebears disappeared?" Stewart repeated.

"Yes, gone from this land," the wolf said. "They were here one day, and gone the next."

So they did escape! "Do you know where they went?" Stewart asked. "Could they have gone back to where they came from?"

"Only they would really know," the wolf said.

"True," Stewart said. Given the strangeness of Bitopia, they could have gone anywhere. "But why did the Venators go too? Aren't they from here?"

"You mean an indigenous creature?" the wolf asked. "Certainly not. I thought they were of your world; they appeared at the same time as the first little ones, grew in number as the little ones grew in number, and left when the little ones left."

"They're not from our world," Stewart said.

"Interesting," the wolf said. "That's a puzzle worth pondering. However, I will save that thought for tomorrow. Now please, you must excuse me, it is long past the time I usually slumber. And if you need the cover of darkness to return to your lair, I suggest you get moving as well. I bid you a good night and safe journey."

Stewart wanted to ask more questions—*Why were they here? Where in the universe was Bitopia?*—but the wolf had already turned and disappeared into his den. No matter. They had found what they had come for. They had a way to defeat the Venators, the same method that the Forebears had used, successfully. And now the words of the Third Prophecy—*stand fast and tall*—made sense. The Forebears had taken a stand, showed no fear, and had won.

At least, standing there in the clearing, that's the way it appeared. But when they turned and headed back to the boat, Stewart realized that finding what the Forebears had directed them to had actually been the easy part. Getting back into the city and using what they had found was likely going to be the biggest challenge they had ever faced.

CHAPTER 26

The return trip downstream was uneventful but tiring. The twin moons had separated again and now the yellow one was winning the race to the horizon. Already the intensity of their colors was fading as daylight was beginning to return to Bitopia. The night was still dark but a thin line of navy blue colored one horizon. The buzzing and chirping of insects and beetles tapered off as the creatures retreated to the undersides of leaves and crevices in the tree bark in anticipation of the coming day.

Stewart and Cora took turns at the oars, exchanging places when whoever was rowing began to feel tired. His arms felt like rubber, his body ached, a blister on his right hand had started bleeding, and he no longer knew when he had rowed long enough as he felt exhausted as soon as his turn started. But he did his best to ignore the pain by concentrating on moving the oars in a steady, rhythmic motion.

While sitting in the back of the boat, keeping a lookout for Venators, Stewart thought about what the wolf had told them. While he knew it made perfect sense, as they drew closer to the city—to the fires, the battering ram, the hundreds of Venators occupying the surrounding fields—his resolve began to falter. How in the world would they be able to stand there without fear and face a horde of charging Venators? And how would they get everyone else to go along? He was so glad that he had

Cora with him to help convince the other citizens. As both a Newcomer and an exile, he doubted anyone would listen to him alone.

They heard the crashing on the gate long before they saw the city, a rhythmic pounding that violated the peaceful quiet of the pre-dawn darkness. Cora was rowing the boat when they rounded a bend and the glow of the bonfires around the city gate came into view. The air was much smokier than when they had left, and it appeared that more fires had been lit. Although they were too far away to see any individual Venators distinctly, Stewart could see a seething black mass swarming the area around the gate.

Cora stopped rowing and turned in her seat. She studied the river ahead, then turned back, resting her arms on her knees and letting the oars' blades float on the water. The boat slowed but kept moving with the gentle current.

"How are we going to get back inside?" Stewart asked in a low voice.

"I'm thinking," Cora said. "We've got to make it back to the port we came out. And the best way to do that is to sneak through the forest riverleft where the Venators first massed, cut across the plain to the trees directly riverback, and then race straight across the plain to the port. With luck, we'll—"

"Cora!" Stewart hissed. "Look!"

About fifty yards downstream, on the bank, in a tree shadow cast by the moonslight, stood a Venator.

"Oh no!" Cora whispered, getting off the seat and huddling down in the boat. She pulled Stewart down too. "They posted a look-out. And he's seen us."

As they watched, the Venator turned, crept up the bank, and disappeared into the trees.

"Great," Cora said, "he's gone to warn the others."

"Let's go back," Stewart said. "We can go inland farther upstream, and circle around."

Cora took in a quick breath. "No, we can't. Look!"

Stewart turned and looked upstream. Along the shore about twenty yards back crept four—no, five—Venators, keeping to the shadows.

"It's an ambush," Cora said. "If we try to turn the boat, the group upstream will charge into the water to block our escape. They want to force us downstream, where I'm sure there's an even larger group waiting. We're trapped."

"Can't we go to the other shore, run away from the city, and then cross farther upstream?"

"I'm sure they've thought of that," Cora said. "They did. Look!"

On the opposite bank from the city, Venators were visible in the shadows of the trees. Stewart looked back upstream at the Venators creeping along the bank. There were Venators on both sides now. They had rowed into a trap for which there seemed to be no escape.

CHAPTER 27

With each passing second, the Venator trap grew more and more inescapable. Rowing back upstream was not an option. Rowing downstream was not an option. Doing nothing was also not an option; the river's current was carrying them downstream. At the moment of the Venators' choosing, the trap would be sprung; a hoard of Venators would rush into the water from both banks and swarm the boat. Even though the outriggers made the boat hard to tip, Stewart and Cora would likely get dragged into the water. Stewart had a chance, as he could swim, but Cora would certainly drown. And that realization is what gave Stewart the idea.

"I know what we can do," he said.

Stewart leaned close and whispered into Cora's ear. Her eyes went wide with fear, but she nodded, knowing it was their only chance.

They huddled in the bottom of the boat, peering over the side now and then to check their position on the river. As the current was strongest in the center, the boat pretty much stayed in the middle. Bands of shadow cast by the trees lay like black ribbons on the water. They drifted into a rather wide band of shadow, the darkness rolling over the boat like a black blanket being slowly drawn up. As soon as the darkness of the shadow reached the back of the boat, Stewart and Cora quietly climbed over the stern and soundlessly lowered themselves into the water. Cora grabbed onto Stewart and he let go of the boat.

Stewart kicked hard with his feet to keep their heads above the water. It was a struggle to tread water silently, holding them both above the surface, and he felt himself tiring quickly. Cora was holding on, much tighter than he would have liked. But neither of them could make a sound or they would be caught. Stewart focused as hard as he could on breathing long, deep, and quiet breaths.

They watched as the boat drifted out of the shadow and back into the moonslight. One of the Venators upstream, on the same side of the river as the city, stopped, grunted, and pointed. For a moment, they feared that their plan had failed, but then the Venators were all moving forward again, creeping along the bank, walking right past the spot where Stewart and Cora were treading water. The Venators continued following the boat until they all disappeared from view around a bend.

As soon as they were out of sight, Stewart started kicking to shore. It was hard going, swimming with a person holding on around his neck, but eventually his feet found the pebbly bottom and they walked, dripping wet, to the bank. Moments later, they heard a tremendous howl and violent splashing in the river coming from downstream. The trap had sprung. Stewart and Cora looked at each other, but neither said a word. They both knew that for the second time that night they had escaped a terrible fate.

They heard the oars banging on the boat, followed by howls of a different tone, higher in pitch, surprised, angry. The Venators must have reached the boat and found it empty. As the Venators had seen them in the boat, they probably knew that Stewart and Cora couldn't have gone far. They heard splashing coming in their direction as well as pounding footsteps. Cora grabbed Stewart's arm and without a word they set off running up the bank and into the trees, hoping that their luck would hold for yet a third time that night.

CHAPTER 28

Fleeing through the woods in darkness was a strange sensation. Stewart followed as close as he could to Cora, who seemed to have eyes like a cat. She ducked and dodged, zipping along an invisible path. Stewart imitated her movements as best as possible, but when he didn't, he was met with a branch whack to the face or a hard knock of a tree trunk to the shoulder. But there was no time to worry about the pain. The Venators were in pursuit.

Stewart and Cora ran through the forest, the footsteps of the pursuing Venators muffled by the sounds of their own flight. Although he had no idea how many there were, Stewart could hear them spread out like a fan behind them. The Venators obviously hadn't seen them, but spread out, they created a wide, sweeping net that would catch them if they stopped.

After running for what seemed like an eternity, the forest thinned and suddenly they found themselves at the edge of the plain, staring out across a portion that lay between the forest and the trees riverback. An orange glow on the horizon illuminated one side of the bushes and shrubs dotting the plain and gave the section of city wall containing the gate a sheen like tarnished bronze. The slamming battering ram sounded like distant thunder.

Stewart and Cora could hear the pursuing Venators behind them drawing closer, so Cora dashed out into the open. Stewart took off behind her, ignoring the protests of his aching legs and burning lungs. They crouched as low as they could without slowing down, dashing from bush to bush. About halfway across, they heard a cry that chilled Stewart to the bone. The Venators had reached the edge of the wood and had spotted them.

Cora surged forward and Stewart, breathing in gasps, tried to match her acceleration but couldn't. He could hear the sound of at least a dozen Venators behind him closing in. The density of the bushes increased as he got closer to the trees, and he found himself weaving around them. Rounding a bush, he realized that Cora was no longer running in front of him. He had lost her. At that moment, his feet went out from under him.

Stewart tried to get back up, but in his panic his feet slipped again on the dewy ground, and once again he fell flat. He heard the pounding of the approaching Venator footsteps. They would be on him at any moment. In one last desperate move, Stewart rolled on the ground as fast as he could until he felt himself roll underneath a bush.

Like a herd of possessed horses, the Venators thundered by and disappeared into the forest. Stewart lay under the bush, panting and listening. The Venators had gone, but he suspected that they wouldn't be gone long. Once they realized he was no longer ahead, they would double back. He had to get into the shelter of the trees.

Very slowly, he crept out from under the bush, crawling on his hands and knees. The day was breaking, and Stewart kept to the shadows as much as possible. At the sound of distant footsteps, he lay flat on the ground, using the long grasses for cover. But it was only a Venator patrol, marching around the perimeter of the wall.

Stewart shimmied and slinked along the ground until he finally made it to the trees. He sat up, leaned back against a trunk, and listened. But besides the rhythmic pounding of the ram, there was no other sound. He had no idea where Cora was, but he figured that she would have gone through the trees until she was as close as possible to the riverback port. So that's where he would go.

Suddenly, a hand slapped over his mouth and grabbed him roughly by the arm. He tried to twist out of the grasp, but when he turned, he saw it was Cora. He almost fell over in relief. She motioned with her eyes deeper into the woods. Stewart looked over her shoulder and saw the Venators, fanned out, creeping toward them. Cora gave him a push on the arm and motioned with her head out into the plain. Oh no, Stewart thought. They were going to make a run for it. The distance they had to cover was twice as far than if they had made it through the trees to a spot directly across from the port, but the Venators were blocking their path.

As silently as he could, Stewart took off running. He and Cora burst out from the edge of the trees and into the plain. A howl erupted from the trees as the Venators spotted them. Heedless now of the bushes and trying to move quietly, they ran as fast as they could directly toward the riverback port. To their left, Venators shot out from the edge of the grove of trees, racing to cut them off before they made it to the wall. Stewart pumped his legs rapidly, like the pistons in a racecar engine. He had never run so fast in all his life.

The Venators were closing fast. Stewart and Cora were getting closer to the undergrowth that surrounded the port. Fifty feet. Forty feet. Thirty feet. But the Venators were faster. Stewart realized in a split second of calculation that he was going to be broadsided by a charging Venator the moment he reached the undergrowth. With no other choice, he stopped short and ducked.

The Venator, grinning hideously at the presumed moment of triumph, cried out in surprise as its momentum and weight carried it sailing past Stewart, its long bony arm sweeping the air right over Stewart's lowered head. At the same moment, Cora, who was running full tilt, collided into Stewart, almost knocking him down. But the push by Cora propelled Stewart forward again and the two of them shot toward the undergrowth. Reaching the line of scritchy bushes at almost full speed, there was only one thing they could do. They jumped.

Stewart and Cora cleared the first few prickly stalks before their legs got tangled in the scritchy bushes farther in and they came crashing to the ground. Heedless of the stinging thorns, they scrambled forward, clawing at the earth, desperate to reach the port.

They finally got to the wall. Cora lifted the port cover and shoved Stewart into the hole. He grasped for the rope and started hauling himself forward with every ounce of strength he still possessed, his elbows and knees scraping on the stone. He felt Cora grasp the rope. She was in. To his relief, the port had not been sealed. They were going to make it.

As Stewart hauled himself forward, he heard shouting coming from the other end of the port. He heard the Princeps' voice, and then Lester's. They were arguing. Something about the port being still open. Stewart realized they had made it back just in time.

But then Cora screamed. Not sure what was happening, Stewart yanked himself forward on the rope, heedless of the cuts and bruises from the stones. But then faces appeared in the port opening ahead of him, quickly followed by the pointed ends of two long poles that brought him to a sudden halt.

"Let me go!" Cora screamed. "Let me go!"

"Let us in!" Stewart yelled at the Defenders wielding the pointed poles.

But the pole ends drew closer. Even without the Venators and Cora behind him, the space was so confining that Stewart couldn't back up. Stewart shut his eyes and pressed his face down against the stones to shield it from getting impaled. Cora screamed again.

"Cora! Stewart!"

Stewart looked up. The sharp sticks were gone and the Princeps' face was outlined by the port opening. Stewart quickly pulled himself through the port and tumbled into the city.

"Cora, come on!" the Princeps shouted. "Pull!"

"They've got my leg!" Cora screamed.

Stewart could see her pulling on the rope with all her strength, but she wasn't moving forward. Her face was red with effort and fear. Stewart wished there were something he could do. But there was no way to help.

Cora held onto the rope, her knuckles white. Then suddenly her eyes grew wide. She screamed, lost her grip on the rope, and was pulled out of the port. Stewart caught glimpses of her amid a frenzied whirring of Venator limbs. And then the door slammed shut and he saw and heard her no more.

CHAPTER 29

Stewart sat back, shocked and stunned. One moment Cora was there, the next she was gone. He squeezed his eyes shut, trying not to think about what was happening to her at the hands of that whole gang of enraged Venators. They would hurt her so badly that... Stewart couldn't bear to finish the thought. They had been so close to making it. And she had pushed him in first. If it weren't for her, he would be the one out there.

A rough hand on his arm brought him out of his shock. Suddenly, he was sliding along the ground. It took him a moment to realize that he was being dragged back to the port by Lester.

"What are you doing?" shouted the Princeps.

"He's an exile," Lester screamed, "and has no right to be in the city. He's going back out."

"But we need to talk to him first," the Princeps shouted, grabbing onto Lester's arm.

"I will not have him in this city!" Lester screamed. His eyes were bulging and wild. To Stewart, it appeared that Lester had lost his mind.

"Please, stop!" the Princeps shouted.

"Sir," one of the Defenders yelled. "The Venators are in the port!"

The rope that ran through the port had gone taut. From the vibrations, it was clear something was coming through.

"I said to release him!" the Princeps screamed, balling her hands into fists.

"On what grounds?" Lester countered.

"Sir, the Venators are in the port!" the Defender yelled.

"The moment he was exiled, he lost his citizenship," the Princeps said, thinking quickly. "Now, in battle, he has breached the wall. That makes him an enemy. According to the law, we hold enemies in the holding cell until trial."

Lester opened his mouth to protest, then closed it. "Fine," Lester shouted in frustration. "Seal up the port!" he shouted at the Defenders.

The two Defenders quickly fitted the end of the port plug into the opening and hammered it into place with large wooden mallets.

Lester released Stewart, who fell down to the ground. They were all breathing heavily, so no one said anything for a moment. Stewart sat propped on his elbows, too exhausted even to scratch at the itches flaring up all over his arms and legs from the scritchy bushes. Then the Princeps knelt down next to him. For a moment, her face reflected fear and sadness, but then its impassive expression returned. She looked at his empty hands.

"So Cora..." The Princeps choked up but then quickly regained her composure. "Cora had been carrying what the Forebears had hidden?"

"No," Stewart said. "The Forebears didn't hide an object. The map in the *Comlat* led to information on how to defeat the Venators."

"You have this information?" she asked, her voice rising in hope.

Lester, who had been gasping like a raging bull, slowed his breathing and went silent.

Stewart told them how the map led to the wolf and everything the wolf had said.

"Wait, wait, wait a second," Lester sputtered when Stewart had finished. "The wolf actually said to let the Venators in? That's crazy!"

"The wolf said that our fear gives the Venators their power," Stewart said. "If we are not afraid, they will lose their power and leave us alone."

"That wolf must be in league with the Venators," Lester said.

"If the wolf was in league with the Venators, he could have just eaten us on the spot," Stewart said.

"This is insane," Lester shouted, throwing up his hands. He turned to the Princeps. "Why are we wasting time listening to this? Throw him in the holding cell. We need to keep building the wall."

"What wall?" Stewart asked.

"We're building a stone wall across the gate and in front of all the ports to stop the Venators," the Princeps said.

"But that will seal us in the city," Stewart said.

"It's the only way to stop them," Lester said. "But don't worry, you'll be going back out as soon as your trial is over."

"But the wolf was right," Stewart said to the Princeps. "We can defeat the Venators. He said that the Forebears did it the same way. That's how they won. If we show the Venators that we are not afraid, even if we pretend to be unafraid, just seeing us unafraid will make the Venators lose power."

"What is wrong with you?" Lester screamed. "They're big, tall, bony monsters who will tear you to pieces! You think by just standing there and looking brave that they're going to turn and walk away? You're, you're, you're..." Lester put his hands to his head, then flung them out in exasperation.

"Stewart," the Princeps said. "Lester is right. We can't open the gate. If they get inside, we're doomed."

Lester leaned his face in close to Stewart's. "They've been hunting us since the moment we arrived in this place," he growled. He stood up and turned to the Princeps. "We don't have time for this. You," Lester said, pointing to one of the Defenders. "Throw him in the holding cell."

The Defender went over to where Stewart sat, grabbed his arms, and hauled him to his feet.

"Come on, Princeps," Lester said, "we have work to do."

Lester turned and headed toward the front gate. After a moment, the Princeps gave Stewart a sad look, then turned and followed. As Stewart watched them go, something about Lester's words, about being hunted from the moment they arrived, made him think of what the wolf had said about the Venators. That they weren't from Bitopia. That they appeared when the Forebears appeared and disappeared at the same time the Forebears did. That when the Forebears faced them and didn't show fear, the Forebears won. "An interesting puzzle," the wolf had said. And suddenly Stewart realized the solution.

"Lester!" Stewart shouted. "The boys from back home who tormented you, who you escaped from at the watering hole and then wound up here, in the river. How many were there?"

Lester stopped and turned. "What does that matter?"

"Because I can tell you something that no one else knows, only you," Stewart said.

The Princeps looked at Stewart quizzically.

"Trust me," Stewart said. "I think I just figured out the key to all this."

The Princeps hesitated, then turned to Lester. "Tell him," she said.

Lester's face scrunched up in disgust. "Two. There were two of them, Biff and Scooter."

"And let me guess," Stewart said. "When you emerged from the river, here in Bitopia, you encountered two Venators, didn't you."

Lester thought for a moment. "You're right. Two Venators did chase me to the city. I was lucky to find the port. But so what? It was a coincidence."

"Princeps, how many tormentors did you have back home?" Stewart asked.

"There were, I don't know, about a dozen," she said.

"And when you arrived here, you first encountered that many Venators, right?"

"Yes," she said slowly. "As a matter of fact, I encountered a whole group of them, about a dozen. I was scared out of my wits. I hid in a forest until they were long gone, then stumbled upon the city. Why?"

"When I got here," Stewart said, "I was chased by three Venators. Back home, I had just escaped from three bullies."

"What, you're saying the bullies followed us to Bitopia and turned into Venators?" Lester asked.

"Maybe not the bullies," Stewart said, "but something did. Somehow, our bullies and the Venators are linked."

"Linked?" Lester asked. "That makes no sense. Nothing followed me out of the river. Nothing doesn't just turn into monsters."

"Hold on a second," the Princeps said, "Stewart may be onto something. Tell me," she said to the Defender holding Stewart, "how many tormentors did you have at home?"

"Four," he replied.

"And when you arrived here, did you immediately encounter Venators?" she asked.

The Defender nodded.

"How many?" she asked.

"Four," he said.

The Princeps looked at the other Defender, standing next to the port. He nodded slowly.

"One bully at home," the Defender said, "and I was chased by one Venator the moment I arrived."

The Princeps turned to Lester, who stood with his arms crossed.

"This has to be more than a coincidence," the Princeps said.

"But nothing came through!" Lester protested. "And monsters don't exist on Earth!"

"And I don't think they exist here either," Stewart said. "According to the wolf, the Venators are not of this world. They arrive when we arrive. When I first got here and bumped into Cora and she realized I was a Newcomer, we immediately started running for her boat. Princeps, isn't it true that whenever a Newcomer arrives, Venators suddenly appear close by?"

"Yes," she said. "All Finders know to get the Newcomers to the city as quickly as possible, that's a rule. But until now, I always thought it was a coincidence."

"According to the wolf," Stewart continued, "when the Forebears disappeared, so did the Venators. So there has to be a link. And think about it—the Venators just torment us, like the bullies back home."

"So somehow because of the bullies back on Earth, there are now monsters here in Bitopia?" Lester asked. "That's crazy."

"As crazy as being stuck on another planet with two moons and no sun and not getting any older?" Stewart shot back.

Lester didn't reply.

"Look, I can't explain it completely," Stewart said, "but there just has to be a link. We arrived here because we were afraid and ran from our bullies. We never faced them. But what the Forebears did to defeat the Venators is right there in the *Comlat*, the Third Prophecy passage that says, 'stand fast and tall.' The wolf told the Forebears to let the Venators into the city and not be afraid. So what would the Forebears have done?"

"They would have opened the gate and...stood fast and tall," the Princeps said.

"They faced their fears," Stewart said. "And overcame them."

"Enough of this!" Lester shouted. "We're running out of time."

"Stand fast and tall," the Princeps said again, nodding in realization.

"Stop saying that!" Lester shouted, putting his hands over his ears. "We can seal off the gate and ports. We have plenty of food. And when the Venators finally leave, we can lower the Gatherers on ropes. We'll haul everything over the wall. It'll be fine, you'll see!"

The Princeps walked over to Lester and put a hand on his shoulder. "Lester, I'm afraid too. We all are. But look what that fear is doing to us. We're sealing ourselves inside the city completely. Even if we could make ropes long enough to lower Gatherers down and haul them up with food, there's no way we'd be able to gather enough to feed everyone. Ropes would break, Gatherers would get hurt or killed, and we'd eventually starve. Don't you see?"

Lester's face went white. "You're not thinking of going along with this," he said, gesturing toward Stewart.

"Let's say that you are right, Lester," she continued, "that the Venators are monsters that live in this world. Our fear of them is putting us on a path that will doom us all. Lester, our fear of the Venators is helping them to win. Our fear gives them power over us. We need to take a stand."

"No!" Lester shouted.

"Lester, the map, the wolf, the fact that the Venators do appear suddenly in the same numbers as our tormentors from home the moment that we arrive in Bitopia," the Princeps said. "It all makes sense."

Lester shook his head, almost violently.

"Lester, you know I'm right," the Princeps said.

"We can hold off the Venators," Lester said. "And when they leave, we can unseal the gate and the ports."

"How?" the Princeps asked.

Lester's eyes darted back and forth. "We can, we can..."

"Lester, we have no iron or steel to pry the stones apart," the Princeps said. "Once we seal the gate and ports, once the mortar sets, they're sealed forever."

"The Inventors," Lester said. "They can figure out a way! There must be a way to harden wood to pry off the stones..."

"Lester, you know that won't work," the Princeps said. "Let's unseal the gate now, before it is too late."

"No!" Lester shouted. "I won't let them get me! I won't." Lester started pacing, quick steps followed by an almost frantic turn. "You want to buy into this craziness, you go ahead. You want to die, go ahead! But not me! Not me! I'll organize my own resistance! I'll rally the citizens! We'll hold off the Venators! You'll see, you'll see!"

Lester turned and ran off into the city. The Princeps, Stewart, and the two Defenders watched him go. They could still hear him shouting long after he had disappeared within the labyrinth of houses and ring walls. The Princeps shook her head sadly, then turned to Stewart.

"Come," she said. "It's up to us now."

CHAPTER 30

The scene at the front gate was chaotic. Citizens were streaming in from all parts of the city, hauling wheelbarrows full of stones or carrying them in their arms. The Masons had created a containment pool in the plaza and were mixing up a large batch of mortar. Defenders and other citizens were quickly and haphazardly piling stones against the barricade of crossbeams, smearing mortar onto them and then tossing them onto the pile, as there was no time to fit and set them correctly.

A bucket brigade had been formed from the water basins in the central plaza to the top of the wall where citizens were dumping water on the Venators in a desperate attempt to slow the battering ram by turning the ground around the front gate into a slick, soupy mud pit. Every now and then the rhythmic pounding on the gate was interrupted by a splash and angry cries as the Venators powering the ram slipped and fell. The air was smoky; the torches that had provided light for the citizens working through the night had not been extinguished, even though the day had brightened into morning.

The Princeps led Stewart across the plaza to the base of the stone pile. Without a pause, the Princeps hopped onto the pile and climbed the slippery stones to the top. She turned, faced the plaza, and cupped her hands over her mouth.

"STOOOOOOOOOOOOOP!" she shouted.

The citizens piling on the stones paused, holding their stones for a moment before putting them down on the ground. The Masons, bent over their containment pool, ceased their stirring and looked up. The bucket brigade, like a conveyor belt with the power cut, slowed, then stopped. The square grew quiet. The only sound was the pounding on the gate, which, following a loud *kerschplop* and an angry cry, stopped as well.

"Citizens, listen to me," the Princeps shouted. "Gather into the plaza, all of you. Those on top of the wall, please come down."

By the dozens, citizens emerged from the tower doors and joined those already assembled in the plaza. The pounding on the gate resumed. The Princeps waited until everyone was in place before continuing.

"Citizens, the Third Prophecy—"

Crash!

"—is wrong."

A collective gasp arose from the citizens.

"The Forebears were not defeated, they—"

Crash!

"—defeated the Venators."

At that, all the citizens began murmuring. The Princeps waved her hand, and it took Stewart a moment to realize that she was motioning for him to ascend to the top of the pile. He made his way up, slipping twice, his hands and shoes gummy by the time he reached her side.

"This is Stewart," the Princeps shouted. "This past night, Stewart and Cora—"

The Princeps had to pause to clear her throat. Stewart forced down a lump in his own.

"—bravely traveled to the Outer Reaches."

They heard a loud *ker-schplop* from the far side of the gate as the Venators with the ram lost their footing.

"They encountered a wolf, a denizen of Bitopia, who not only told them that the Forebears defeated the Venators, but the secret to doing so," she continued. "Sadly, Cora did not make it back. But this is the secret that Stewart learned."

The Princeps turned to Stewart. He suddenly felt very self-conscious. He hated public speaking, and there were hundreds of people looking up at him. He took a deep breath and cupped his hands to his lips.

"Citizens," Stewart shouted, his voice sounding funny to his own ears, thin and high-pitched. "The wolf said that the Venators get their power from our fear. The more we fear them, the more powerful they become. To take away their power, we must show them that we are not afraid. Even if we simply *appear* to be unafraid—by not running, or getting angry, or showing them that they bother us—they will lose their power. You might still be afraid on the inside, but show no fear on the outside. That is what the Forebears did, and we can do it too. That's what the wolf said."

At that, the citizens all started talking loudly. Stewart had the sinking feeling that what he said didn't make much sense. He wished that he could explain it like the wolf had.

"Citizens!" the Princeps shouted. "As the wolf has revealed to us, only by showing the Venators that we do not fear them can we defeat them, once and for all. Now listen carefully."

She paused and waited until there was complete silence.

"We are going to show the Venators that we are not afraid. We are going to do what the Forebears did and stand fast and tall."

The citizens started murmuring again, the sound higher in pitch: nervous, fearful.

"We are going to rip down this stone pile!" the Princeps said. "We are going to let them into the city. We will stand fast and tall and show no fear!"

The roar from the citizens was almost deafening. Shouts of "No!" and "You can't do that!" punctuated the din.

"Citizens, I know you are afraid," the Princeps said, waving her hands to quiet everyone down. "I am too," she said when the noise subsided. "But if we stand together, if we stand as one, we will defeat the Venators once and for all. Are you with me?"

The Princeps' words were met by silence.

"Are you with me?" the Princeps repeated, even louder.

Again, silence. To his horror, Stewart realized that no one was going along with the plan.

"Good citizens," the Princeps said. "I know that this is the hardest thing that has ever been asked of you, to stand and face that which you fear most. But let me tell you this."

She paused until there was complete silence.

"As your Princeps, you have protected me and ensured my safety at the expense of your own. Gatherers, you have gone outside the wall for me, taking great risks to keep me fed. Masons, you have toiled with stones and mortar to shelter me. Defenders, you have faced down the Venators in battle while I remained safely behind you. But now I am going to be the one standing in front of you."

At that, the crowd started murmuring.

"So strong is my conviction," the Princeps continued, raising her voice above their chatter, "that we can stand fast and tall and face down this threat, these Venators, our fears, that I will be the first to face them."

The noise of the crowd grew, and the Princeps waited. After about a minute, she raised her hand for silence.

"But I can't do this alone. If we are to be victorious, we must stand together. Trust in me that what I have told you is true and I pledge to you that we will be victorious. Who will stand with me?"

No one said a word.

"Who will stand with me?" she asked again.

The only sound was that of the Venators on the other side of the gate.

Stewart looked at the Princeps. Her face remained impassive; however, he saw in her eyes, for the first time since arriving in Bitopia, uncertainty.

"This has never happened before," the Princeps said, so quietly that only Stewart heard. "They've always done as I've asked. Everything I've done since the beginning has been in their best interests. I don't understand."

Stewart stared out at the citizens. For over a hundred years, the Princeps had been their trusted leader. And now, when it mattered most, they were refusing to follow. Their fear, Stewart realized, was greater than their faith in her. The power to overcome that fear, Stewart realized, could only come from one place: within.

"I rowed a boat last night," Stewart blurted out, so suddenly that even he was surprised by his words. The crowd went completely silent. For a moment, he felt extremely self-conscious, and wished he hadn't opened his mouth. But he certainly couldn't say that he had rowed a boat and leave it at that.

"I rowed a boat on the river," Stewart continued. "I'd never done that before. And as I rowed, I watched the two moons, the pink one and the yellow one, make their way across the sky. They chase each other. Did you know that? When you see them from down here in the city, you don't get to see that. I went swimming, too. Do any of you remember swimming?"

Silence.

"You know, the feel of cool water, floating, kicking with your feet and moving your hands, feeling the water slip through your fingers?"

A few hands went up.

"I had forgotten how wonderful swimming can be."

There were a few murmurings from the crowd that sounded like agreement.

"I saw a creature called a unideer," Stewart said. "It was a like a deer from back home, just smaller. It had come to the river to drink. It was beautiful. And I listened to the birds and bugs chirp and chatter, not the sound echoing within the wall of the city, but their pure voices. I felt soft grass under my feet. I smelled the scents of fields and forests. I heard water rippling over rocks in the river.

"Do any of you remember running in fields, playing in a forest, rolling around on the grass, seeing deer, listening to the birds, being on a river, doing anything like that?"

Most of the citizens raised their hands.

"I know many of you haven't been outside the wall since you got here," Stewart continued. "I can tell you that it's a beautiful and wonderful world out there. And I only saw a small part of it. But despite being out there and doing all those fun things, I ran back here, back inside the wall. And do you know why?"

No one answered.

"Because I was afraid," Stewart said. "I was afraid of the Venators and so I came back inside. And coming back inside the wall made me realize something, not just about me, but about each one of us."

He paused. The crowd went completely silent.

"We all arrived in Bitopia because of our fear," Stewart continued. "Each one of us feared our tormentors back home and chose to run from those fears instead of facing them. And that's how we got here. By running and hiding, we lost home. If I had chosen to confront the bullies that I ran from back home, to show them that I wasn't afraid of them, I would not be here. But I didn't, and so here I am. Here we all are.

"And look at us now. Here we are in an amazing world, with wonderful and beautiful creatures and places to explore, just like we had at home, and all we've been doing is hiding, hiding because of our fear. Just like at home.

"And now, with these stones we're piling in front of the gate and all the ports, we're sealing ourselves into this city, forever losing any chance of exploring this incredible world. We're once again going to lose an amazing world.

"So I ask you all this: how many wonderful worlds do we have to lose before we learn to stop running and hiding from what we fear?"

Stewart scanned the crowd. All eyes were locked on him.

"How many worlds?" he asked again.

Silence.

"I don't really know what will happen if we confront the Venators," Stewart continued. "But I can tell you this: I'd rather take a chance on confronting the Venators and face my fear than risk losing Bitopia forever. One day outside the wall is worth more than an eternity trapped within."

A murmur arose from the crowd.

"I know that confronting your fear is one of the hardest things to do," Stewart said, raising his voice. "You won't find the strength to do it because a wolf tells you. You won't find the strength because the Princeps asks you. And you won't find it because I, or anyone else, tell you it's worth it. You can only find it if *you* want to. And I know that you want to. We all want to. No one wants to be trapped in here any longer. We've already lost home; we can't afford to lose Bitopia.

"The only way to break free of this wall is to break free of your fear. If you want the chance to run around outside and explore the world, to not lose Bitopia forever, then come forward and pick up a stone off this pile. Just one stone."

No one moved.

"Just one," he said again.

The crowd was perfectly still.

"One stone is all it takes," Stewart said.

Stillness.

Stewart's heart sank. This was their only chance at breaking free. Now they would be trapped in the city forever.

Then a movement in the crowd caught Stewart's eye, and his hopes rose. Someone was coming through the crowd from the back of the plaza. But then Stewart saw the head of curly red hair. It was Lester.

Lester pushed forward until he reached the base of the stone pile. He looked up at the Princeps and Stewart, then turned and faced the crowd. What was he doing? Stewart wondered with growing fear. Was he going to try to convince the citizens to stand with him? Was he going to organize his resistance? If so, then all would be lost. Stewart looked over at the Princeps, who appeared to be holding her breath.

For a long moment, Lester stood silently. All eyes were on him. Then Lester turned, bent down, and picked up a stone. He held it high over his head so everyone in the crowd could see it.

Was he going to launch into a speech, about the strength of stone and the need to keep adding to the pile? Stewart wondered. He could hardly breathe. Their fate, like that stone, was in Lester's hands.

For another long moment, Lester stood before the crowd. Then, without saying a word, Lester turned, carried the stone to the side of the gate and tossed it against the base of the wall. A moment later, a girl at the front of the crowd reached down and picked up a stone. Then a boy pushed through the crowd and grabbed a stone. Three girls stepped forward together and each picked up a stone. Before long, all the citizens started coming forward, picking up stones, and carrying them to the side of the gate.

Stewart's heart leapt. He turned and found the Princeps looking at him with a smile on her face. Stewart blushed. The Princeps then descended the stone pile and, when she reached the bottom, made her way through the crowd until she found Lester, and gave him a hug. They exchanged a few words, and Stewart saw Lester smile. He was back on their side.

Stewart descended the pile and joined the Princeps, who had returned to pick up a stone. They both grabbed a stone and carried it to the side. Around them, the other citizens were busy carrying the stones and piling them on either side of the gate. Before long, the large mound of stones that the citizens had piled against the barricade of crossbeams had been removed.

The Venators had broken through the wood of the doors and were now slamming into the crossbeams. With the stones gone, the crossbeams shook with each hit of the ram. Lester gestured to a dozen Defenders, and they raced into the towers. Moments later they appeared at the top of the wall and lowered down ropes. Defenders down below secured the ropes to the top crossbeam and it rose up and away from the gate.

It's happening, Stewart realized. The barricade was being removed. In just minutes, the Venators would be in the city.

The Princeps, meanwhile, was moving about the crowd, giving reassurances. She was smiling and laughing and patting shoulders. Stewart knew she was putting on a front, but the effect that it had was remarkable. Fearful faces became hopeful. One citizen actually smiled at another. Everyone seemed to stand straighter. That everyone was afraid, there was no doubt. But it was remarkable how calm everyone looked given that, at any moment, the Venator army was going to come charging into the city.

The Princeps walked to the front of the crowd, directly opposite the steadily shrinking barricade. She reached out her hands, taking those of the closest citizens. One by one, all the citizens joined hands. Stewart took the hands of citizens on either side. Before long, all the citizens were joined together.

Slowly, the crossbeam timbers rose up. Soon the top of the doorway was visible. More crossbeams were removed, and the gap between the top of the doorway and the top of the barricade widened. The pounding of the ram, meanwhile, had stopped. Another crossbeam went up, and the gap widened further. Suddenly, Venators' bony hands appeared on the top of the next crossbeam. Moments later they were scrambling over the timber wall and running straight for the citizens.

CHAPTER 31

Seeing the Venators charging toward them, Stewart could only think of one thing: *Run!* His mouth had gone dry and his knees started to tremble. He was standing a few rows from the front line of citizens, and the Venators were charging at full speed. But there was no place to run, no way to escape. Stewart closed his eyes.

He felt his arm get yanked as the Venators plowed into the line of citizens. He almost lost his grip on the person next to him, but the person on the other side held him up. Then more Venators crashed into them and everyone fell down. Stewart struggled to his feet and found himself face to face with a Venator. He stood frozen with fear but tried not to look afraid, expecting the Venator to grab him at any moment. The Venator stood staring at him. Stewart put on the bravest, meanest expression he could. The Venator turned and lumbered off.

Stewart felt a rush of elation. He had done it! He had faced down the Venator by showing no fear! It was so easy! He looked around at the other citizens. Some were standing fearlessly in front of Venators, just like he had, but others were scuffling with them. Wait—why were they scuffling?

Then Stewart saw the Venator he had faced down. It stood in the plaza, scanning the citizens. It zeroed in on one of them, a boy, and rushed toward him. Stewart suddenly realized why the Venator had turned and walked away. Stewart hadn't actually faced him down; the Venator had the wrong person. Each Venator was the embodiment of one *specific* person's fear, and it went looking for that one person. And if *that* one Venator went looking for *that* boy, Stewart realized with growing horror, that meant...

Over the din of shouting and shoving and cries of the citizens, Stewart heard a loud growl directly behind him. He turned and found himself face to face with a Venator. No, not one, but three of them. He knew immediately that they were the same ones who had chased him into the city. They were *his* Venators.

One of the three Venators howled, then leaned forward and gave Stewart a shove so hard with its bony hands that he felt like he had been hit in the chest by a fistful of flying rocks. Stewart fell backward, his fall cushioned by a boy who was already sprawled on the ground. Stewart scrambled to his feet, and the three Venators moved in. Stewart tried to look unafraid, tried to suppress the fear he felt welling inside, tried to stand tall and confident, but his body began to shake. He locked his muscles, standing as rigid as possible, but he couldn't stop. And, worse, he saw that the Venators could see it. In a flash, one of the Venators reached out, grabbed him, and lifted him off his feet. Stewart felt as though he were going to faint.

"Why are you doing that to him?" came a loud voice from somewhere nearby.

Stewart turned his head. The boy that he had fallen on was standing behind Stewart, off to one side, and was pointing at the three Venators.

"Why don't you leave him alone?" the boy asked.

He's helping me, Stewart realized. He didn't know this boy, yet the boy was acting like a friend. And although the Venators weren't that boy's Venators, they appeared, to Stewart's surprise, to be listening to him.

"Are you mad at him?" the boy asked.

The Venator holding Stewart looked from the boy to Stewart. Stewart braced himself for whatever cruel punishment the Venator holding him intended to inflict. But then, to Stewart's great surprise, the almost gleeful sneer on the face of the Venator holding him slowly disappeared. The Venator lowered him back down to the ground and released him.

What just happened? Stewart wondered. Did the Venator let him go because the boy had talked to it? Had no one ever tried talking to the Venators?

A nearby commotion caught Stewart's attention, a scuffle between a Venator and one of the bigger Defenders. The Venator pushed the Defender, and the Defender did his best to hold his ground. But when the Venator tried to shove the Defender again, the Defender knocked the Venator's hands aside. Although the Defender was only half as big as the Venator, the Venator paused, not sure what to make of the Defender.

The next moment, Stewart found himself sprawled on the ground, the side of his head aching and his ear ringing from a hard blow. He felt a wave of dizziness, and all around him everything fell silent, as though he were watching a movie with the sound turned off.

Bewildered, he pulled himself up onto all fours. He looked over at the Defender, who stood facing the Venator, neither moving nor backing down. Then Stewart looked over at the boy who had spoken to his Venators. He stood calmly, now and then his mouth opening as he spoke to a nearby Venator. And whatever Venator he spoke to stopped and stood still.

Why weren't the Venators bullying *them*, knocking *them* down? They had been in the plaza before the Venators came charging through the gate and hadn't moved when Stewart had first asked everyone to pick up one stone. They had been just as afraid, if not more afraid, than Stewart. So what were they doing that Stewart wasn't?

Then Stewart realized the answer. The Defender and the boy were doing more than just showing no fear. They were both standing up for themselves. They didn't just stand there and take it. And until Stewart did that, he realized, until he calmly but firmly stood up for himself, he was always going to be the one on the ground.

In a crescendo of sound, Stewart's head cleared and the noise around him returned to his ears. Stewart got to his feet and turned to the source of the punch. One of the three Venators stood before him. The Venator smiled and stepped forward to shove Stewart.

Stewart knocked the Venator's bony arms to the side. "Stop it!" he said forcefully, trying not to let his anger show. "You have no right to do that! Leave me alone!"

Stewart stood defensively, ready for whatever the Venator might do next, and stared at the Venator, trying to appear calm and confident. He braced himself, expecting some form of response, but the Venator just stood there, seemingly puzzled. Then, to Stewart's surprise, the Venator stepped back. At that moment, in seeing how the Venator reacted when he stood up for himself, Stewart's fear of the Venators, and their power over him, was gone.

"Waaaah...ooof!" *Splat!*

Stewart turned at the sound. A few feet away, a boy had been shoved by a Venator and had landed in a sitting position in the mortar basin. He sat with a curious expression on his face, no doubt a result of the unexpectedly soft and squishy landing.

The nearby Defender started to laugh. The boy who had yelled at Stewart's Venators also started to laugh. And the boy sitting in the mortar started to laugh as well. Before he knew it, Stewart found himself laughing.

Other boys and girls around them, engaged in confrontation with Venators, heard and looked over to see what was so funny. And they started laughing too. Soon the laughter was spreading among all the citizens.

The effect on the Venators was stunning. One after another, the Venators stopped their torments and just stood there. Then the most incredible thing happened. The Venators, who were standing as still as stone, started to grow lighter as though being drained of color. As the citizens watched in amazement, the Venators grew more and more transparent, until they were just an outline and then, in a blink, they faded completely.

And Stewart suddenly understood the link between their bullies on Earth and the Venators. It wasn't that something had followed the citizens through the portals into Bitopia; rather, it was what they had brought with them: fear. The Venators were the embodiment of the citizens' fear, the fear of their bullies. And when the citizens' fear ceased to exist, so did the Venators.

The citizens laughed harder. The sound carried out beyond the front gate and, as the citizens watched through gaps in the timbers, the Venators still outside slowly began to grow transparent and then they too faded to nothing. Within moments, the entire Venator force had disappeared.

Like a dam bursting, the citizens erupted into a cheer. Stewart raised his face to the sky and shouted with glee.

CHAPTER 32

Stewart stood in the plaza in almost joyous shock. Citizens were cheering and laughing, even those with bloody noses and scraped knees. Some were reenacting their encounters with the Venators, showing how they shoved or got punched but stood right up again.

Stewart smiled and turned in a slow circle, taking in the full height of the wall encircling the city. Millions of stones held together by thousands of pounds of mortar were not as strong as the citizens standing up to their fears. Never again would they need the protection of the wall.

Stewart felt something brush his cheek. Something in the air had changed. Other citizens felt it too and the laughter and cheering slowly died down to silence. The air of the city was moving. It was almost imperceptible at first, but then it developed into a faint breeze that grew stronger and stronger. Stewart realized that the cold, damp, heavy air in the city was rushing out through the front gate, draining out of the city.

The remaining crossbeams were lifted away and the citizens slowly started for the opening. The force of the air rushing out through the gate was strong. Stewart picked his way carefully across the mud puddle, walking on the ram and broken pieces of the gate doors. He stepped out onto the plain, blinking against the brightness, feeling the light of day on his skin. He looked back at the gate, watching the faces of the citizens, many of whom hadn't been out of the city since the day they arrived in Bitopia, take on expressions of wonder.

And then he understood the meaning of the last line of the Third Prophecy, *then scatter with the wind;* like the Forebears, they had walked through the gate with the rushing air. And they were free. Free from fear. Free to roam the land. Free to explore. Free to experience the delights and hidden wonders of Bitopia. Free to just run around and play. They were no longer citizens in a society ordered to ensure survival, but instead had become children once again. Sure, there were things out there that could hurt them, but it was far better to explore and experience everything the world had to offer than to hole up in the dark and damp city, imprisoned by the wall, imprisoned by fear.

Stewart's thoughts were interrupted by a shout. Someone pointed across the plain. A lone figure was moving toward them. It was small, not a Venator. It was a girl. Cora!

With his heart leaping with joy, Stewart took off running toward her. She was walking slowly and with a limp, but otherwise she appeared okay. When he was close enough, she waved and smiled. Stewart couldn't believe it.

"Cora! You're alive!" Stewart said, running up to her. He couldn't resist giving her a hug.

"Looks like you are, too," she said.

"But I saw you get dragged out of the port," Stewart said. "And all those Venators! What happened?"

The Princeps and Lester came running up.

"You're okay!" the Princeps said.

"The wolf was right," Cora said. "The Venators pulled me out, but I didn't run. I actually fought my way to my feet and then started shouting at them. For the first time, instead of being afraid, I got mad. I stood my ground. And then they just—*poof*—disappeared! It was the strangest thing. I tried to get back in through the port, but it was plugged. So I went and sat in the forest to wait, figuring that you would soon defeat the Venators. And here you are."

They all laughed with relief and talked about the battle as they walked back to rejoin the other children. Many of them were standing around the front gate, almost in a daze. Others were inspecting the nearby bushes or smelling flowers. Some were venturing farther out into the plain.

A piercing scream shattered the silence. Stewart's heart jumped into his throat. Had he been wrong about the Venators? Had they rematerialized for a counterattack? Was their disappearing act just a ruse to draw the citizens out into the open?

Then he saw it. Standing in the middle of the plain was a wooden door. It was not the kind used for the entryway of a house but rather one that looked like it belonged on an antique wardrobe. It hovered in the air, as though the rest of the wardrobe was invisible. And the girl that had screamed was standing before it, shaking, with tears streaming down her face.

A portal! Stewart realized. As everyone watched, the girl reached up and, with a shaking hand, pulled open the door, revealing a dark opening. The girl stepped inside and pulled the door closed. The moment it closed, the door disappeared. The girl was gone.

That was her portal, Stewart realized, the way she had come to Bitopia. And that explained what must have happened to the Forebears. Facing their fears and defeating the Venators was the key to getting the portals to reappear, the key to getting home.

For a moment, no one said a word. Then screams erupted from the children, screams of delight mixed with tears, hope, and anxiety, and they started running in all directions. Doors, barrels, and even trees that didn't grow in Bitopia had appeared all over the landscape. Children were racing toward them, recognizing the portal that could take them home. Children were disappearing by the minute. Some ran right to their portal while others stood, pensively for minutes on end, staring at the way home and steeling themselves for what they would find on the other side. A few children hung back, saying goodbye to friends and giving hugs, before turning and dashing off to find their portal.

Lester, his eyes wide, turned and, without saying a word, walked toward the river. He waded into the water and disappeared beneath the surface. For a split second, his form was visible just under the ripples, but then a moment later he disappeared.

Stewart stood with Cora and the Princeps, watching the children go. They were disappearing by the dozens. Before long, only the three of them remained.

"So that's that," the Princeps said. "I guess conquering our fear freed us from more than the city." She turned and looked at the wall. "Funny how what I called home for so long looks so dreadful and uninviting from out here. Well," she said, turning back to Stewart and Cora. "There are no more citizens, so I am needed here no longer. From now on, I'll just be Evelyn." She laughed. "Take care, both of you."

The Princeps turned and walked briskly across the grass, heading straight for a single door that stood in the plain. She opened it and stepped into the opening.

"Wait!" Stewart shouted.

Perhaps thinking that Stewart was saying goodbye, the Princeps waved. A moment later, she and the door were gone.

"What is it?" Cora asked.

"The *Comlat!*" Stewart said. "Remember what the wolf said? We need to write better instructions on how to find him."

"She's gone," Cora said. "It looks like it's up to us. But do you think we need to?"

Stewart looked up at the towering wall of the city. "As much as I'd like to think that we're the last ones to ever inhabit that city, something tells me that others will arrive after we've gone. And they're going to need the same help we did. We should probably fix the gates and open the ports, too; the wall won't be any protection if whoever comes here next can't get in or keep the Venators out."

Stewart and Cora went back into the city. It was strange to be inside with all the citizens gone. The streets were empty, quiet, eerie. And the wall; what had been a cherished source of safety and protection for so long now seemed like a useless old husk. And Stewart found it stranger still how he suddenly didn't mind being there now that he knew he could get home any time he wanted.

At the Curia, Cora retrieved a charstick from the Princeps' office. They were about to head out to the Vault when Stewart remembered his clothes. He certainly didn't want to return wearing the Bitopian garb. He found the room with his clothes and changed.

At the Vault, they carried the stone vessel safeguarding the *Comlat* out into the light, then carefully removed the book. Stewart laid it on the lid and opened it to the last page, the map.

"Do you want to do it?" Stewart asked Cora.

"You do it," Cora said. "It's been a few decades since I wrote anything."

Stewart suddenly realized why the map had no labels; the Forebear who made it had probably forgotten how to write.

Cora pushed on the plug at the end of the charstick, forcing out some of the black charcoal paste, and handed it to him. He took the charstick in his hand and paused. There wasn't much space. What should he write? He thought for a moment, then, next to the dot, wrote:

THE WOLF CAN SET YOU FREE

Then he closed the book, returned it to the vessel, and put the vessel back into the Vault.

Since they didn't know how long it would be before anyone else arrived, they decided to seal the Vault to protect the *Comlat*. They retrieved a few wheelbarrows of stones, still wet with mortar, from the front gate, and stacked them as carefully as they could over the door. Their work was not perfect, but at least the *Comlat* would be better protected.

Next they went to the Woodshop, gathered up planks, mallets, stone-tipped augers, and wooden pegs, and dragged the materials out to the front gate. As best they could, they placed the new planks over the broken sections of the doors, drilled holes, and attached the planks with pegs. When the doors were relatively solid, they pulled them closed and secured them with a few planks.

As the light of day dimmed, they walked the interior perimeter of the wall, visiting each port and knocking out the plugs. When all the ports were open, they both took one last look around the quiet city, then, without a word, pulled themselves out through a port.

"So where's your portal?" Stewart asked after they had made their way past the scritchy bushes and were out in the open field.

"That way," Cora said, pointing to the forest riverleft. She looked worried.

"Cora, it will be okay," Stewart said.

"But what if I have no relatives left?" she asked, fighting to hold back tears.

"Then you can come live with me," Stewart said.

"Really?" Cora asked, sniffling.

"Of course. We have plenty of room, and Harrison City is a nice place to live. Lots of trees, like this place. You'll love it. And I could use a friend."

Cora smiled. "I'd like that."

"Then it's decided," Stewart said. "As soon as you get back to New York, call me and let me know how things are. You know what a phone is, right?"

She thought for a moment, jogging her memory, then nodded. Stewart told her his number and made her repeat it ten times.

"But in case you do forget the number, my address is: Stewart Owens, 17 Elm Street, Harrison City. You can use the address to look up my number in a directory. And so you know, the date is..." Stewart thought for a moment, calculating the days that had passed, and then told her the date. "Got it?"

Cora repeated all the information a few times so she was sure to have it memorized. "Okay," she said. "I've got it. I guess I'll talk to you soon." She gave him a hug, then turned and, without looking back at the city, headed toward the forest.

Stewart watched her go, then headed riverright toward the hill to find the drainpipe.

CHAPTER 33

Stewart walked through the pipes, taking them at random. He didn't care where he came out, as long as it was in Harrison City. He decided that at the first manhole cover or drain he came to, he would just sit and yell and wait to be rescued. It no longer mattered what kind of trouble he would get into. No one would believe what actually happened to him, so he would just say that he bumped his head and got knocked out. At the very least, he might get some sympathy and a reduced jail sentence.

Stewart came to a junction and let out a shout. Sitting on the gravel in the mouth of a pipe was his backpack. He had found the pipe that led to the drain.

Stewart grabbed his pack and ran forward. To his great relief, the street repair work had not yet finished and the grate was still off. Ignoring the splattered mess covering the drain pit bottom and the sticky goo coating the rungs, he raced up the ladder and ducked under the yellow tape.

Right into the hands of Frankie, Dirk, and Judd.

"Had enough of the bombardment, huh?" Frankie asked, grabbing him by the arm.

Stewart stared at them in shock. It was days ago that he went down in the drain. How in the world were they still next to the drain the moment he popped up?

"Now about that pack," Frankie said, slowly reaching for it with his free hand.

Stewart felt a jolt of fear and started to shake. This was it. They were going to get his coins. Dirk and Judd leaned their tall, spindly forms in closer, menacingly. Like Venators.

Stewart yanked his pack away from Frankie and pulled his arm out of his grasp.

"Why don't you guys just leave me alone!" Stewart said. He said it so loud that the bullies flinched.

"Who do you think you are?" Frankie said, recovering from his surprise.

"Yeah, we're the Rage," Judd said.

Dirk gave Stewart a shove. Stewart stumbled back but remained on his feet. He was frightened, but he knew if he showed it now, he was doomed.

"The Rage," Stewart said, his attempt at a forced laugh sounding like a hoarse cough. "What is that? What does that mean? It makes no sense."

"It means..." Judd started to say, then he looked at Dirk. "You made it up. What does it mean?"

"You know, the Rage," Dirk said.

"No, I don't know," Judd said.

"What do you mean you don't know," Dirk shot back.

Seeing them momentarily distracted, Stewart pushed past them. "I'll let you guys work this out. I have things to do."

"Where do you think you're going?" Frankie asked, lunging and grabbing Stewart's shirt.

Stewart knocked his hand away. "Why is it that you guys always follow me around?" he asked. "Doesn't

226

'the Rage' have anything better to do than follow sixth graders?"

Frankie's mouth twisted into an angry snarl. "Yeah, we do have better things to do," he said. "Like this."

He gave Stewart a shove that sent him sprawling. Stewart rose slowly to his feet, holding his elbow, which had banged on the concrete, his face twisted in pain.

"Whaddaya gonna do, cry?" Frankie asked, sneering.

Stewart looked at him, the corners of his mouth drooping. Then he burst out laughing. It wasn't that his elbow didn't hurt. It wasn't that he was certain the bullies were going to leave him alone. To be honest, he had no idea what they were going to do. Rather, he realized that he had always seen them as monsters, but in reality they were just older boys who enjoyed the power they got from scaring others. In seeing them for what they really were, Stewart no longer felt afraid. The bullies had lost their power.

"What is wrong with this kid?" Judd said, walking angrily toward Stewart. "Let me show you what the Rage—"

Just then a woman came out of the deli, carrying a bag. Judd stopped short.

"Oh, excuse me, boys," she said. She saw how the bullies were standing, and how Stewart was holding his arm. "Is everything here all right?"

Had it been any day in the past, Stewart would have said that he was new in town and lost and needed help finding his way home so the adult would save him from the bullies. And the bullies now seemed to be expecting such a response, for Frankie snorted in disgust.

Stewart looked at Frankie, then at the woman. "Everything's fine here," he said. "There's no problem."

The woman nodded and went on her way. Stewart stood there, alone, on the sidewalk, facing the bullies. He braced himself for whatever they might do next. But then, to his surprise, they turned, climbed on their bikes, and pedaled off.

CHAPTER 34

Stewart's pace quickened the closer he got to home. He knew his mom would be worried sick. She would have called the police, the fire department, all the area hospitals, and would even have hung "lost boy" signs all over the neighborhood with his picture. And he knew which one she would have chosen, the awful one taken at the department store portrait studio when they first came to Harrison City, where she made him wear that dorky striped shirt.

When his house finally came into view, though, he stopped short and stared. There were no police cars in the driveway as Stewart had expected, only his mom's blue sedan. The street was empty of news vans with big channel numbers on the sides and telescoping antennas rising high above the roofs, parked at the ready to report breaking news about Stewart's disappearance. No posters with Stewart's picture and phone number had been taped to trees or telephone poles. As a matter of fact, the house looked exactly the same as when he left it. The neighborhood was quiet and still, with only the birds chirping in the trees to break the silence.

Stewart's mom was in the kitchen preparing dinner when he entered the house. But she didn't run to meet him and sweep him up into her arms as Stewart figured she would. Nor did she have the stern, serious expression that meant he was in trouble, as Stewart feared she might. In fact, his mom expressed surprise that he was home so early and went back to washing a zucchini.

"Early?" Stewart asked. "Are you sure that I'm early and not really, really late?"

"Look at the clock," she replied.

"But didn't you miss me the last couple of days?" he asked.

His mom laughed, thinking he was playing a game. When Stewart asked what they had for dinner last night, she told him baked ziti and Brussels sprouts, which is exactly what he had eaten the last night that he was home. She didn't even express dismay at how dirty his face was or how tired he looked. She just laughed at his insistence that he had been gone for longer than a day and finally told him the game was over and, because he was so filthy, to take a bath before dinner. Stewart started to protest, but gave up.

It didn't make sense, he thought, as he climbed the stairs to his room. Everything looked the same, and was the same, as if he had been there as recently as that morning. How could that be? He stopped in front of the mirror and saw the slightly red bruise on the side of his face from where the Venator had hit him.

The doorbell rang, and Stewart's mom called up the stairs for him to get it. He ran downstairs and opened the door to find an express deliveryman, holding a cardboard mailer.

"Stewart Owens?" the deliveryman asked.

"Yes, that's me," Stewart said.

"Sign here."

He held out an electronic signature device and handed Stewart a digital pen. Stewart scribbled his name on the line, then took the envelope and closed the door.

"Who was that?" his mom called from the kitchen over the noise of the water running in the sink.

"Special delivery, for me," Stewart said.

"Who's it from?" she asked.

Stewart looked at the return address. "I don't know, a bunch of last names."

He looked closer at the address and his eyes grew wide. It was from New York. He yanked the tab that opened the mailer and pulled out a single sheet of paper. It was a letter, on fancy letterhead: *Meyers, Stegman, and Cohen, Attorneys at Law*. He started reading.

Dear Mr. Stewart Owens:

Per the directive of our late client, Mrs. Cora Williamson, please find below the text of a message she wished to have delivered to you on this date. If you have any questions, please do not hesitate to call us.

Best regards,

Donald Stegman

Dearest Stewart,

I hope this message finds you well. When we parted, I had accepted in my heart that all my family and friends were deceased, so imagine my surprise to find that I returned to New York at the exact same moment that I had left! And how I surprised Velma and her gang when I jumped out from behind the trash barrel dressed in my Bitopian clothes!

While I was so happy to see my family, friends, and especially Spritz, I had been so looking forward to seeing you again. However, I fear that is not to be. I wish you all the best and a wonderfully long, healthy, and prosperous life, just as I have had. Always remember, show no fear!

Warmest regards and your friend in spirit always,

Cora

P.S. Just as I promised, the first chance I got, I learned how to swim!

Stewart read over the letter again, tears welling in his eyes, and then put it back into the mailer. So Cora had returned to her family. That explained why no time had passed. Everyone must have returned home to the exact same moment that he or she had left. Although he felt sad that he would never see her again, he smiled at the memory of all they had endured and achieved in Bitopia.

CHAPTER 35

The next day at school when the recess bell rang, Stewart followed his fellow students outside. Old Miss Wupplemeyer was already in position, and Stewart headed toward her and the spot where he usually sat, against the school building. He walked into the shadow of the wall and stopped short.

The wall. He had been living in his own Bitopia, he realized, using the safety of the wall and the proximity of the playground monitor as protection. Out on the playground, there was a whole world to explore, games to play, and friendships to make. Sure, the bullies were out there, but had he forgotten so soon the words of the wolf and Cora's reminder?

"Show no fear," he said aloud.

With a mix of trepidation and joy at the possibilities, discoveries, and challenges that awaited, Stewart turned and walked out of the shadow of the wall and into the sunshine of the playground.

ACKNOWLEDGMENTS

I would like to thank the following individuals for their invaluable help with this book:

Kristen Kilpatrick, 5th-grade teacher at the Mill Pond School in Westborough, Massachusetts, for reading an early version of this book to her class and providing a wealth of feedback from her students.

Alyssa Eisner Henkin, agent at Trident Media Group, for guidance and suggestions on the opening chapters and the dialogue.

Julia Magnusson, my editor, for taking on the manuscript and giving suggestions that greatly improved the story.

Megan Arendt, the most voracious reader I know, for reading multiple drafts of the book and pointing out missing elements, straightening out confusing passages, and providing insightful feedback on revisions.

Israel C. Kalman, noted school psychologist, psychotherapist, lecturer, author, bullying expert, and creator of the *Bullies to Buddies Golden Rule System*, for providing guidance and suggestions on the characters' actions in the bullying scenes.

Esther Piszczek and **Robin Fradkin Matthews**, for their early rounds of editing.

Christine Eskilson, Joan Bernard, and (again) **Esther Piszczek**, my writing group readers, for all their questions and suggestions over the years that helped get the first few drafts into shape.

Greg Marathas, artist and illustrator, for having the tremendous talent that created the book's cover and the professionalism that made the process of creating it so enjoyable.

Natalie Prochnow Mauceli, for so thoroughly proofreading the manuscript.

And last, but not least:

Kathleen Magnusson, my mom, who read the manuscript more times than anyone and pointed out various sentences to "fix and smooth" which resulted in no fewer than one hundred and twenty-seven changes to the text.

ABOUT THE AUTHOR

Ari Magnusson spent his first year of high school getting picked on by a huge bully until the day he figured out the secret to stopping him. They eventually became friends. Ari lives in eastern Massachusetts. *Bitopia* is his first novel.

Published by
OLIVANDER PRESS
Boston, Massachusetts
Olivander, Olivander Press and associated logos are
trademarks of Olivander Press LLC.

This is a work of fiction. All characters, names, events,
places, and incidents are products of the author's
imagination or used fictitiously. No reference to any real
person is intended or should be inferred.

Library of Congress Control Number: 2011961142

eISBN-13: 978-0-9848610-6-4
Paperback ISBN-13: 978-0-9848610-5-7
Library Binding ISBN-13: 978-0-9848610-4-0

First edition - February 2012

Printed in the United States of America

Cover illustration by Greg Marathas
Cover image copyright © 2012 by Ari Magnusson

G4

CPSIA information can be obtained at www.ICGtesting.com
Printed in the USA
LVOW121530150513

333966LV00018B/690/P

9 780984 861057